BABY, IT'S WARM OUTSIDE

CHRISTMAS KEY BOOK SIX

STEPHANIE TAYLOR

For Aunt Bev—
One last "oy vey!"
Until we meet again...
-S.

"But that is what islands are for; they are places where different destinies can meet and intersect in the full isolation of time."

— LAWRENCE DURRELL, BITTER LEMONS OF CYPRUS

DON'T MISS OUT ON NEW RELEASES...

Want to find out what happens next in the Christmas Key series? Love romance novels? Sign up for new release alerts from Stephanie Taylor so you don't miss a thing!

Sign me up!

1

MAIN STREET IS DRIPPING WITH HOLIDAY SWAG. THICK, GLITTERING ropes of tinsel are wrapped around every lamppost, and strings of colorful lights twinkle around the doorways of every business on the street. Shop windows are decorated around their edges with a dusting of white snow from a can, and miniature potted palm trees dot the sidewalk, each tree covered in shiny ornaments in every color of the rainbow.

"We need more red and gold," Holly Baxter says, standing in the middle of the street with a clipboard in hand. She's surveying the scene in the dim evening light and watching as her friends and neighbors dig through the boxes of decorations she keeps in storage so that they can add more holiday-themed decor at any time of the year.

"You want red and gold on the lampposts?" Fiona Potts asks. She's standing in front of A Sleigh Full of Books in a pair of cutoff shorts, hands in her back pockets as she surveys the tangle of glitter and lights that have turned Christmas Key's Main Street into a simulation of Disney's Magic Kingdom at Christmastime.

"Just more of it everywhere," Holly says.

"Hey, Holly." Miguel Cruz drives up behind her in the B&B's golf cart. He pauses next to the mayor as she checks something else off on the clipboard. "The dock is decorated and lit up. It's probably visible from Key West."

He's kidding, of course—Key West is fifty miles to the east of Christmas Key—but Holly likes the image of her island sending rays of holiday cheer and light into the night that can be seen from a distance.

"Perfect. Thanks, Miguel." Holly's eyes flicker in his direction and then back to her clipboard again as she consults the next item on her list.

Miguel's only been living on the island for a month now, but he's already fallen into the rhythm of daily life on Christmas Key like he's been there for years. He'd come with a group of construction workers to help build the new (and brightly decorated) dock so that bigger boats could visit the island, and had quickly realized that it was a place he might like to stay. The idea of having a full-time handyman and jack-of-all-trades on the island had appealed to both Holly and her uncle, Leo Buckhunter, and as co-owners of the island, they'd agreed to make it happen and give Miguel a job.

"I'll head over to the B&B and make sure it's looking the way you want it to," he assures Holly. "When I left, Bonnie and the triplets were setting up for the party and turning the dining room into Santa's Workshop."

"Thanks, Miguel," Holly says, giving him a grateful smile. At twenty-three, Miguel is young and strong and nimble, and has the kind of energy Holly needs to get things done.

As much as she loves and adores her neighbors, their advancing ages sometimes slows things down—but not much. It never ceases to amaze her how quickly everyone is ready to roll up their sleeves and get to work on whatever project or scheme Holly cooks up; even the oldest islanders are flexible and open to change as she works to expand and develop Christmas Key.

"I've got the wreaths," Buckhunter says, walking past his niece with four artificial holiday wreaths looped over each arm. The greenery is flocked with fake snow and tricked out in colorful bits and bobs, and they look like gigantic bracelets snaking their way up his arms. "One on each door here?" he asks, nodding at the shops on Main Street.

"Yes, please." Holly puts a check mark next to "hang wreaths" on her list.

The event they're decorating for this weekend is important to her for a lot of reasons. First of all, it's the christening of the new dock, built specifically for Island Paradise Excursions to bring boat loads of visitors to the island for day and weekend trips, and secondly, it's the first time Holly and the islanders have put on a murder mystery event, and she's coordinated with Vance Guy—proprietor of the island's only bookshop—to bring in a famous author of mysteries to join them.

"Sugar, sugar, sugar!" Bonnie Lane shouts, rushing down the front steps of the B&B and doing a fast sashay down the street in Holly's direction. Her fire-engine red hair is teased into an updo, and her lips are painted hot pink to match the thin pink sweater she's wearing. Her ample chest is draped with a string of silver tinsel that she's wound around her neck like a scarf, and she's got jingling bell earrings dangling from each earlobe.

"What's up, Bon?" Holly can hear the fevered pitch of her office assistant's voice, but the long list of things she still needs to accomplish keeps her from jumping on Bonnie's train of excitement without hearing more.

"Jantzen Parks just texted me. ME!" she squeals in her southern accent. "Look at this, doll." Bonnie holds out her phone and turns it so that Holly can see the message.

Holly smirks. "Well, you *did* give him your personal number and tell him to let you know what you could do to make his stay more comfortable."

Jantzen Parks, the mystery author who's coming to the island, is right up Bonnie's alley. Tall and distinguished, with richly silvered hair and a neatly trimmed goatee in the photo that smolders from the back cover of each of his novels, he's captivated Bonnie entirely as they've prepped for his arrival.

"I know, honey," Bonnie says, toying with one end of her tinsel scarf. "And he just texted to tell me that he's looking forward to meeting me and thanking me personally for making all of his arrangements."

"Good grief." Holly rolls her eyes. "I hope he knows what he's in for."

"And I hope he's looking for inspiration for his next book's leading lady," Bonnie says, waving one hand through the air theatrically. "I can see her now: red hair, the kind of supple bosom that a man just can't keep his eyes off of—"

"Oh, jeez," Holly interjects.

"—a bottom as ripe as a Georgia peach, and the personality of a firefly crossed with the crackling sunset of an autumn evening."

"An imagination as vivid as a rainbow over the ocean..." Holly adds as she makes a gagging face.

Bonnie's laughter fills the street. "Oh, sugar! I love you." She leans in and gives Holly a perfumed hug. "You're something else."

"No, Bon, *you're* something else," Holly says, hugging her back tightly. Given her tenuous and fraught relationship with her own mother, and the easy, loving bond she shares with Bonnie, it's no secret to anyone on the island that the older woman in her arms is the mother Holly *wishes* she had.

"The dining room looks amazing," Bonnie says, switching gears. "And I have it all set up with Calista and Vance for the boys to come and visit Santa there before anything crazy happens."

"Good." Holly was unsure at first about the idea of including Santa and Mrs. Claus in the murder mystery, but the company she's hired to put on the event have assured her that it's going to be a fun game, and that they'll give the only two children on the island ample time with Santa before the actual murder mystery begins so that they'll get to enjoy the magic of the season without being privy to any part of the game.

"And I have everything set up as far as lodging. We've got some empty bungalows around the island that we're using for this weekend, and the B&B is stocked, cleaned, and ready for guests. Everyone has a bed to sleep in, and I've got your packets all printed and ready to hand out at the village council meeting first thing in the morning."

Holly takes a deep breath and blows it out slowly. It's been a ton of work to put this together, but from the time she decided to put on a murder mystery weekend, she'd gone into planning mode and devoted all her energy to making a Christmas-themed event happen in the middle of December. This way, all of the decorations will be up, the kind of holiday cheer that only comes with the real approach of Christmas will be in full-swing, and the weather will have pleasantly lodged itself somewhere in the wintery mid-70s.

"Okay, after we're done with decorations, let's meet up in the office and go over the packets one more time," Holly says.

The light from the large picture window of the B&B's office shines out onto Main Street, and from where they stand, Holly can see both of their desks, lit by two small lamps. On the window sill sits a row of flameless candles shaped like sturdy candy canes, their electronic lights flickering cheerfully.

"You got it, boss," Bonnie says with a mock salute. "I can't wait to find out what roles everyone is playing in this murder game. This is going to be so much fun!"

"Bon," Holly says seriously, "we can't know what roles everyone has—we have to be in on the game, too."

Bonnie's face morphs into a theatrical frown. "Oh, come on, Holly Jean. Let's just take a little peek—no one will know!"

"Uh uh." Holly shakes her head. "We may have done all the planning and behind-the-scenes setting up, but when it comes to this murder, I want it to be as much of a mystery to us as to everyone else."

"Oh, fine. You're such a stickler for rules." Bonnie pulls a mock pout and turns to head back to the B&B's dining room. "I'll meet you in the office when you're done!"

Holly watches her go, shaking her head as Bonnie waves flirtatiously at Wyatt Bender, still holding the end of her tinsel as she wiggles her way up the stairs.

No matter what kind of event she stages, or what natural disaster washes up on the shores of their tiny island, Holly can always count on the reassuring sameness of the people she shares her life with. And she does. She counts on it and she loves it and she wouldn't trade a second of it for anything else in the world.

"Fiona?" she calls out, watching as her best friend tosses a ball of tangled mini-lights at Cap Duncan. He catches the lights and tucks them under one arm. "More red and gold!" she reminds her. "We need *lots* more red and gold!"

2

THE DINING ROOM OF THE B&B IS CRAMMED FULL OF LIVER-SPOTTED islanders wearing plaid Bermuda shorts, pastel golf shirts, and sun visors. Mixed in amongst them are the growing handful of younger locals, like Katelynn Pillory and her sixteen-year-old son, Logan; Officer Jake Zavaroni; Vance and Calista guy and their six-year-old twin boys, Mexi and Mori; and Miguel, who is the island's only twenty-something.

"Let's have everyone come to order as quickly as possible," Holly says from behind her podium. She raps her light pink marble gavel against its block gently, trying to get everyone to settle in and turn their attention to her. "We've got a lot to cover."

"You've got a bit more to cover than the rest of us, Mayor," Maria Agnelli says, perching gingerly on the edge of her front row seat. She holds up a gnarled finger and wags it around, indicating Holly's denim skirt and the tight black tank top she's wearing over her yellow bikini. "You got a sweater or anything you can put over those ta-tas?"

Holly laughs good-naturedly. Mrs. Agnelli has always been the most cantankerous islander. Everyone tolerates the octogenarian's sense of humor and colorful words, though she's grown a touch more persnickety and outspoken—even for her—in recent months.

"She looks lovely, Maria," Millie Bradford says, sliding into the seat next to Mrs. Agnelli's. "If I still had a figure like hers, I'd run around this island in nothing but a few leaves held together with some string and a prayer."

"She already does," Mrs. Agnelli retorts, tugging at the hem of her ironed blouse primly.

Holly chooses to ignore the entire exchange and to instead focus on the task at hand. As mayor, she decided long ago that her wardrobe should always include a bathing suit of some sort beneath her clothes, because the opportunity to take a swim in the pool or the ocean at some point during the day might just present itself. She tucks the yellow string of her bikini under the strap of her tank top and gives the block another whack with the gavel.

"I've got paperwork to hand out here, and I know you'll all have questions," Holly says, motioning for Bonnie and for Heddie Lang-Mueller to join her up front. The two women walk down the aisle with stacks of manila folders in hand. They stand next to Holly at the podium. "Bonnie and Heddie have all the paperwork here to prepare us for our very first murder mystery weekend, and I'm really excited to get things underway."

A hush washes over the crowd as they get ready to hear more about the event that's going to take place in less than twenty-four hours.

"Before we give each of you the information that's specifically tailored for you and your role in the game, I wanted to go over the things you'll find in your packet." Holly switches on her laptop and an image comes to life on the screen behind her via a small projector. "Okay, first of all," she says, turning to look at the slide that's displayed. "We have your murder mystery kits complete. In them, you'll find the following: a guest list, so you know who everyone is; a page with information about the game; some character background to help you understand who the key players are, and a list of items we need for the scavenger hunt that will take place at some point."

Heddie and Bonnie move through the crowd, passing around the envelopes with each individual's name written across the front in

Bonnie's neat script. A ripple of laughter moves through the room as people start to read the game instructions.

"Santa Claus?" Wyatt Bender says, a smirk on his tanned face as he reads through the information. "This is a holiday-themed murder mystery?"

"Oh no," Calista says, standing up slowly with the papers in her hands. "I hope this doesn't scare my boys, having Santa involved in a murder—even if it is fake."

"Calista," Holly says, holding up a hand as people start to talk louder, protesting against anything as unwholesome as including the institution of Santa Claus in a murder mystery. "I've already gotten reassurance from the company that we can have a full Santa visit for the boys right here in the dining room before anything related to the game happens."

She motions around the heavily decorated dining room, and everyone looks at the red velvet chair with gold-painted wood that's been set up for Santa in one corner. The room is draped with tinsel and ornaments just like Main Street, and a tree stands near the French doors that divide the dining room from the lobby, its branches laden with sparkling baubles so that it twinkles under the overhead lights.

"And you're sure nothing will scare them?" Calista holds the paper to her chest, a worried expression on her pretty face. "They still believe in everything related to Christmas."

"Hey, *I* still believe in everything related to Christmas," Holly says. "And I can promise you, they will have no idea any of this is going on as long as you don't talk about it in front of them."

"Did you pick this particular game?" Iris Cafferkey raises her hand from the center of the room. "It's pretty funny, lass," she says in her thick Irish brogue, "but it's a tad dark. Do the guests know what they're in for?"

"Oh, most definitely. Island Paradise Excursions specifically advertised this as a holiday murder mystery, and everyone who signed up is open-minded and ready for a good time, which is exactly what we're going to give them."

Ever since pitching the idea of building a new dock in conjunction with Island Paradise Excursions, Holly has been looking forward to the day the boat will pull into port, so to speak, and deliver a group of eager tourists to the island to fill up the B&B's rooms and to drop their money into the coffers of all the island's businesses. The arrival of the boat tomorrow means that Christmas Key is on the map again as far as tourism, and Holly can't wait to have new people amongst them for a long weekend of fun and mystery.

"Hey, it sounds great to me," Jimmy Cafferkey says from the seat next to his wife. "You can count us in for whatever roles this murder mystery outfit wants to assign to us."

"Which is my next point—thanks for the segue, Jimmy." Holly switches the slide on the screen to the next one. "Each of you has either been assigned a specific role to play in the mystery, or you're going to just play yourselves, but with the expectation that you'll participate alongside the other guests who come in on the boat. No one in this room knows exactly who will be murdered, how it will happen, or why. The solution to this game is as much a mystery to all of us as it is to the people who aren't here yet. Only the company putting on the event knows the exact details to solve the crime."

"So what's the big secret?" Cap Duncan pipes up. He's leaning his tall frame against the wall on one side of the dining room, his own paperwork in one large hand, which he waves around as he talks.

"The secret is that we aren't going to talk with one another about who we are. If you've been given a specific character, you need to consider the costume this person might wear, what sort of things they might say and do, and how you can incorporate yourself into the game while staying in character."

"Of course we can keep the secret," Maria Agnelli says impatiently. "There's hardly anything there to wag our tongues about."

Holly forces her eyes not to wander to the faces of Maggie Sutter or Logan Pillory, two of the people responsible for spreading around confidential information a few months back when Kitta Banks and Deacon Avaloy had chosen Christmas Key as the location for their top secret wedding. The loose lips on the island had nearly sunk things for Holly, but in the end, both Kitta and Deacon had been so happy with their fun-filled nuptials that they'd been willing to overlook the transgressions as part and parcel of being famous and newsworthy.

"Yes," Holly says carefully, "I believe you can keep your roles under your hats. I know we're all on board to make this an amazing and fun weekend, and if you have any questions at all, I want you to call me or come by the office anytime so we can be the best hosts who ever threw a murder mystery weekend."

The crowd breaks up instantly, and voices ricochet around the dining room as people talk about the mystery. Holly steps out from behind the podium and walks over to where Jake is standing. He's reading his character information.

"Do you think you're up for the challenge of acting like a police officer in this charade?"

"Well, I think I can manage the costume, at least," he quips. His eyes dance as he looks at Holly. "This is some event you're putting on, Hol. I'm impressed."

Holly and Jake have had some real ups and downs in their relationship over the past two years, but they're currently in a very comfortable and platonic place, and Jake has been spending time with Katelynn Pillory, which Holly has slowly grown accustomed to.

"Thanks. I feel like we've really been trying some innovative things. I'm excited to start using the new dock, too."

"Definitely. This is a step in the right direction. I'm all in for this game, and if I can do anything else to help out this weekend, just let me know." Jake reaches out and squeezes Holly's shoulder before making his way to the doors of the dining room where Katelynn is waiting for him. Holly waves at her old friend, and Katelynn waves back with a smile.

Holly *has* tried some innovative things of late, and she's got to give herself credit for that. From her first foray into eco-tourism with a group of fishermen from Oregon to the reality show that she'd lobbied to have filmed on their beaches, and from a pirates' weekend to the Hollywood wedding between Kitta Banks and Deacon Avaloy,

Holly has really gotten creative. And, as always, she has to credit her neighbors for helping her to make it all happen. As she watches, the islanders stand around chatting and laughing.

Holly walks through the lobby to head back to her office. Jantzen Parks is set to arrive on a smaller boat later in the evening, and she needs to get him all set up at A Sleigh Full of Books so that he can start prepping for his reading there.

Sitting in the chair that faces her white wicker desk, Holly looks out at Main Street at the colorful, over-the-top Christmas decorations juxtaposed against a bright blue winter sky. Not for the first time, she reminds herself how lucky she is to live in such a beautiful slice of paradise. In the midst of her blissed-out spell of gratitude and island love, her desk phone rings.

"It's Fiona. You better come on out here—I'm in front of Jack Frosty's."

"What's up, Fee?"

"Mrs. Agnelli just took off her shirt and threatened to spend the whole weekend in a bikini if you didn't assign her a better role in the murder mystery."

"Oh, lord." Holly stands up abruptly and closes the lid of her laptop. "I'll be right there."

3

MIGUEL IS HOLDING UP A GIANT BEACH TOWEL PRINTED WITH PALM trees and coconuts in front of Mrs. Agnelli as Holly rushes down the steps of the B&B and out onto Main Street.

"I'm in a bathing suit, you ninny," Mrs. Agnelli says. "Holly, this is a protest. I'm trying to speak my piece here." Maria Agnelli shouts a string of curse words in Italian and tries to swat Miguel away.

"Mrs. Agnelli." Holly takes the ends of the towel from Miguel gratefully and wraps them around the older woman's shoulders. "It's December, and sometimes you get chilly in August. Let's get you covered up."

"Don't treat me like I'm old, Holly Baxter," she says, though she lets Holly lead her over to Jack Frosty's. "I'm getting tired of a few things around here and I just want to be heard."

"So come to my office. There's no reason to be out here in—" Holly moves the towel and peeks at the bathing suit that Mrs. Agnelli is wearing. It's pale pink and low-cut, and about a mile and a half of deeply freckled cleavage stares back at her. She re-wraps the towel. "There's no reason to be out here looking like a *Sports Illustrated* swimsuit model."

Mrs. Agnelli gives a *humph* of disapproval. "I'm no swimsuit model," she argues. "And we both know it. But you walk around here all day with your suit on like it's underwear, just showing it off, so I thought if I did the same thing I might get a little attention."

If the crowd on Main Street is any indication, she's gotten more than a little attention. Holly steers Mrs. Agnelli to a table inside her uncle's open bar/restaurant and gets her situated in a white plastic chair.

"Hey, Buckhunter?" Holly calls out to her uncle. "Any chance we can get a couple of iced teas here?"

"You got it," he says casually, not even acknowledging the scene that's just played out right in front of his establishment. He drops the wet towel he's been wiping the bar with and starts to whistle the tune to "Copacabana" as he pours their drinks.

"Now," Holly says, turning her attention back to Mrs. Agnelli. "What is it that you want to protest? What's your ultimate goal here?"

As if she hadn't truly thought out her platform before unbuttoning the rosebud-covered blouse that had covered her skimpy swimsuit at the village council meeting, she puts a knobby hand to her chin and ponders the question.

"Well," she finally says. "First of all, I want to have a role in this mystery weekend. I got nothing."

"You didn't get *nothing*," Holly says gently. "You're an islander. You get to be yourself. Preferably the Mrs. Agnelli who walks around fully-clothed, but you get to be you."

Another *humph* from Mrs. Agnelli.

"Having enough islanders is important to the game," Holly says, reaching out and putting her hand over Mrs. Agnelli's. "We need you. But if you could be another character, who would you be?"

"I want to be the person who gets murdered."

Holly sucks in a breath. "Mrs. Agnelli, why would you want to be involved in the murder? That's so...dark."

"It's so exciting!" she counters. "And I'm never involved in any excitement around here. The closest I've come is a couple of dust-ups with that floozy Idora." She's referring to a string of small (non-physical) tussles she's had in the past couple of months with Idora Blaine-

Guy, one of the island's newest residents and grandmother to Mexi and Mori. Idora had come to the island earlier in the year to help look after her twin grandsons and to keep them out of mischief while their father opened up Christmas Key's first bookstore.

"I don't understand what's going on between you and Idora," Holly says, resting her elbow on the table and putting her chin in her hand. "Can you explain?"

"She's just snooty," Mrs. Agnelli says. "That's what she is. Flirts with all the men, walks around with her chin in the air, and acts like she's better than all of us because she's got her kids and grandkids here on the island."

"And I would argue here that Bonnie flirts with all the men, and you have no issue with that."

"Bonnie's a friendly tart," Mrs. Agnelli says, pounding the tabletop lightly with a shaky fist. "It's hard to hate a friendly tart, even if she does wiggle her bottom too much."

Buckhunter is standing over them with two glasses of iced tea in his hands. His goatee twitches with repressed laughter.

"Well, Idora keeping her chin in the air might just be good posture," Holly says, moving on to the next topic. "And she is pretty lucky to have her family here, but then again, they are why she's even on the island in the first place."

Mrs. Agnelli drinks her iced tea through a straw and watches the crowd as it disperses on the street. "Yeah, I guess so." Her voice has gotten softer, and the fire seems to have gone out of her belly. "But I still want a more exciting part in the game."

Holly drinks her own tea and considers this. The game isn't really hers to alter, but what the people do on the island during the event is definitely up to her. She watches Buckhunter move around behind the bar, still whistling "Copacabana" like he doesn't have a care in the world.

"I've got a great idea," Holly says. She catches Buckhunter's eye and motions him over. "Jack Frosty's is right next door to the B&B. Why don't we create a special role here for you."

"Like what?" Mrs. Agnelli's eyes narrow with suspicion and

curiosity. Buckhunter is standing behind Mrs. Agnelli shaking his head and giving Holly a look that's meant to stop her before the train leaves the station entirely.

"Like as restaurant hostess."

Buckhunter's head shaking ramps up and his eyes widen.

Holly warms to the idea. "That way, as the details of the crime unfold, you'll be right here. You'll see who goes in and out of the B&B, you'll hear the gossip as you seat people, and you'll be able to keep an eye on the main suspects."

Mrs. Agnelli nods as she considers this idea. "Okay," she says. "I can see that. Maybe. Can I wear a costume?"

Buckhunter's face is turning red and Holly is afraid he'll say something to squash the idea, so she reaches out and puts a hand on his arm.

"You could wear that Hawaiian print shirt I have," Holly offers.

"And one of your little denim skirts?" Mrs. Agnelli arches an eyebrow. "I bet we wear the same size."

Holly swallows a laugh. "Sure, you can wear one of my skirts, too. We'll have you work—when is a good time, Buckhunter? The night of the murder?"

"And the next day, too," Mrs. Agnelli adds. "I need to be here to see the action and to hear everything."

"Do I have a choice?" Buckhunter looks at Holly incredulously, though beneath the irritated face, she can see mild amusement. "I've never had a hostess here."

"I'll be the best damn hostess," Mrs. Agnelli promises. "You'll want to hire me on full-time."

"Let's just take these first two days and see if we can survive them." Buckhunter shoots Holly a look and walks back over to his bar.

"This is a pretty good role," Mrs. Agnelli says, standing up with the towel wrapped around her shoulders. It's fallen open enough that her wrinkled chest is visible again. "I'll come by your place later to borrow that outfit."

"It's okay, I can bring it to you," Holly says, standing up to face her. Her bungalow is on the most wooded and untamed part of the island, and she isn't keen on Mrs. Agnelli bumping down the unpaved path, dodging branches and stopping for marsh rabbits or overfed geckos. Pushing Mrs. Agnelli's golf cart out of a pothole isn't on her list of fun things to do today. "I'll run home and get it and have it with me at the B&B later on, okay?"

"You got it, Mayor." Mrs. Agnelli heads toward the stairs on her slightly bowed legs, reaching out to hold onto the railing as she descends to Main Street and totters off.

"I could kill you," Buckhunter says as he sets clean glasses on a shelf behind his bar. "And if this is a total nightmare, I just might." He winks at her to let her know he's kidding.

"You better watch yourself, Buckhunter," Holly says, pointing her finger and holding up her thumb like it's a gun. "Or you might become our number one suspect in this game."

He rolls his eyes. "I'm shaking."

THE SMALL BOAT CARRYING JANTZEN PARKS ARRIVES AT THE OLD DOCK right at the end of Main Street an hour before sunset. Bonnie has very helpfully offered to greet him alongside Holly and Vance, so the three of them stand there, watching as the famous author disembarks with a single bag in his hands.

"Good evening," Jantzen says, stepping from the boat onto the dock. He's about six-foot-five and wearing spotless, perfectly creased khaki pants and navy blue boat shoes. Over a white polo shirt with its collar turned up, he's slung a blue and yellow striped sweater, which is knotted around his shoulders. "The welcoming committee, I presume?"

Holly is slightly awed by his imposing presence and by his magazine-perfect outfit. She feels even more starstruck than she had by Kitta Banks, the Oscar winning actress whose wedding she'd planned and saved from certain disaster two months before.

"I'm Holly Baxter, mayor of the island." She steps forward and extends a hand. His hand clasps hers gently, but his shake is firm.

"And I'm Bonnie Lane," Bonie says with a kittenish bat of her lashes. "It's *such* a pleasure to finally meet you, Mr. Parks."

"Please, call me Jantzen," he says, eyeing Bonnie approvingly as he hangs onto her hand for just a beat longer than necessary. "And this must be Mr. Vance Guy," he booms, turning to Vance and clapping him on the shoulder with one hand as he shakes with the other. "It's always a pleasure to meet a fellow book lover and a purveyor of literature."

"Welcome to the island. We're thrilled to have you," Vance says. His big, white smile makes it clear how excited he is to have a well-known author visiting his bookstore.

"Let's get you to your room at the B&B so you can get settled in before the event this evening," Bonnie says, waving at Jantzen so that he'll follow her.

"I'm going to set things up in the shop," Vance says, pointing at the bookstore. "I'll see you back there in a while?"

"Certainly," Jantzen says, carrying his small bag in one hand like it weighs nothing. "I'll just find something to eat and be right over."

"Are you hungry?" Bonnie asks in a concerned voice. "Because we've got some lovely spots to grab a bite. I'd be happy to show you..."

Holly stops where she is and watches as Bonnie's hands flutter around her pretty face. Her pores ooze sex appeal. It's an amazing thing to watch when Bonnie Lane turns up the heat to red-hot, and the way men respond to her is no less fascinating to Holly. Jantzen Parks is looking down at her with open interest, his free hand hovering right behind Bonnie's back as if he's the one guiding her.

They disappear into the B&B to get Jantzen all checked in, and Holly stands on the sidewalk, taking a deep breath of the evening air. As she does, the timer-controlled holiday lights kick on all up and down Main Street, bathing everything in a warm, Christmasy glow.

❅

"I want to thank you all for coming tonight," Jantzen Parks says. He's sitting on a stool on the back deck of A Sleigh Full of Books beneath strings of the clear twinkling lights that Vance Guy has strung through the trees. "*Murder on Marco Island* is my eighteenth book set in the great state of Florida, and I'm so happy to have the chance to come to Christmas Key and meet you all."

Bonnie is perched on the edge of a chair right up front near Jantzen Parks. Holly watches with amusement from her spot in the doorway as Bonnie uncrosses and recrosses her legs in Jantzen's line of sight.

"This is really exciting," Vance says to Holly from behind her shoulder. He's holding several copies of *Murder on Marco Island* in his arms that he's hoping to get the author to sign and the locals to buy. "Jantzen even told me that he'd sit down with me at some point this weekend and talk about agents and publishers." Vance has long been working on a novel of his own, and the idea of getting to pick the brain of a successful author is clearly one he relishes.

"I'm happy for you, Vance." Holly's arms are folded and she's leaning against the doorframe, hugging her light green sweatshirt around her as a slight winter breeze blows across the deck.

"*The sand from the beach was gritty beneath her feet as she walked through the darkened entryway,*" Jantzen reads, holding a hardcover copy of his own book open in his hands. He clears his throat and looks out at the small crowd from over the top of his reading glasses. "*It wasn't until Margaret nearly tripped over the body on her kitchen floor that she realized the sound of her maid's vacuum was missing. The house was silent. Through the open door that led to her balcony, she could hear the waves crashing on the beach. But there, on her floor, was the glassy-eyed body of her younger sister, Eleanore.*"

Holly has to admit that it isn't groundbreaking material, but having an author there in their midst, reading aloud a part of his own work, is pretty impressive.

Because the dining room of the B&B is already set for the murder mystery event the next evening, and because not everyone on the island is interested in attending Jantzen's book reading, Holly has decided to forgo a big dinner at the B&B in Jantzen's honor and instead encouraged Vance to send everyone over to the Ho Ho Hideaway for drinks and snacks and Joe Sacamano's live guitar music after the reading.

"Hey, Holly," comes a whispered voice. It's Miguel, peering through the open doorway of the bookstore from Main Street. Because the shop is long and narrow, his words carry and she turns around from her spot at the back door.

"What's up?"

"Sorry to interrupt." Miguel waves her over.

Vance has turned off the overhead lights and has just the lamp on his table in the corner switched on, plus the holiday lights in his front window. The lights from the back deck cast a warm glow on the hardwood floors of the darkened shop.

"It's okay, I was just listening," Holly says. "Do you read his books?"

"Uh, no," Miguel admits once they're out on the sidewalk. Jantzen's booming voice follows them through the shop and they can hear him reading even out on the street. "I only read books about sports."

"Sports?"

"Yeah," Miguel says. "You know, like books where a football team comes together and overcomes some obstacle. Or biographies of famous baseball players. Stuff like that."

"Hey, you like what you like, right?" Holly says. "My favorite books are usually about impossible romances that sometimes don't have a happily ever after."

"That sounds depressing," Miguel laughs.

"Eh. It's like real life, isn't it? You win some, you lose some."

"True, true." Miguel shifts from foot to foot like he isn't sure what to say next.

"Did you need me for something?" Holly asks, thinking of the set up he's been doing for the murder mystery weekend. As the island's resident handyman, Miguel has been on call for everything from plumbing and electrical disasters to general holiday decorating needs, and she assumes he's called her away from the book reading over something related to the big weekend event.

"Actually," he says, kicking at an invisible rock with the toe of one shoe, "I was wondering if you were going to the Ho Ho after this."

"To the Ho Ho? Yeah, of course. I'll be there. How about you?"

"I'm not sure." His chin is lowered and he squints up at her like he isn't sure he should say anything. "I've been really happy here this past month, and everyone's been...pretty cool. But sometimes I feel like they think it's weird to see me during off-hours having a beer when I'm the guy who unclogs their sinks and fixes their shutters."

"What?" Holly actually laughs out loud. "Has anyone made you feel that way?"

"No, no." Miguel waves a hand and shakes his head. "I think it's all me—it's my problem. I just can't get over it."

"Well, you're going to have to," Holly says forcefully. "This island is too small for you to pretend like you don't live amongst the rest of us. And no one expects you to. You buy your groceries at the Gift Shop, you grab a burger at Jack Frosty's, and you pick up a morning coffee at Mistletoe Morning Brew. I *promise you* no one thinks anything of it. All of us who work here also live here and do the things everyone else does."

Miguel scratches his head. "Yeah, I see your point...but I'm also the only person here who isn't white. Except the Guys—I almost forgot about them."

Holly thinks about this for a second. Vance and Calista and Idora and the twins are the only black people on the island. "You're right. I never even consider that, but you are right." What might that feel like to be such a small minority of the population that you don't even have another person around you who comes from where you come from? Holly has no idea. "I don't think anyone else here even speaks Spanish."

"Jake does—at least a little." Miguel smiles at her. "He had to learn some, being a cop in Miami."

"I forgot about Jake." Holly frowns. "But we need to fix that."

Miguel shakes his head again and gives an embarrassed laugh.

"No, we don't need to fix anything, Holly. It's not that. I guess sometimes I'm just...homesick."

"I've been homesick before, so I do hear you," Holly says. She'd taken a trip to Europe earlier in the year that had only served to reinforce for her how much she loved her life and her home. "I want to think about this more, but I feel like we can come up with something that might not only help you feel more at home here, but also let us into your world a bit, you know?"

"I don't want to be any trouble, Holly, you know that. I'm grateful to be here. This is all in my head—I promise you."

"Come on, Miguel. Ideas are already knocking around in this melon," Holly says, rapping her skull lightly with one fist. "Before you know it, I'll have something planned and you'll be totally amazed. Just give me a little time."

"Okay, okay," Miguel says. As he laughs, two deep dimples pierce his smooth cheeks. "But in the meantime, what would you say to letting me tag along with you to the Ho Ho?"

"Miguel," Holly says, putting one hand on his shoulder and looking him squarely in the eye. "You're not tagging along with me anywhere." His face falls until he realizes that Holly's not done talking. "Wherever I go, we go together."

4

OUTDOOR SPEAKERS ALL UP AND DOWN MAIN STREET ARE PLAYING "IT'S the Most Wonderful Time of the Year" as Holly and a handful of helpers bustle around, making last minute adjustments to decorations and sweeping the sidewalks.

"We've got twenty minutes!" Holly calls out, sliding behind the wheel of her hot pink golf cart. She pulls away from the curb and rounds the bend on December Drive, heading towards the new dock at Candy Cane Beach. The first boat from Island Paradise Excursions is scheduled to arrive by two o'clock, and Holly is more than ready to get the murder mystery guests over to the B&B and get things started.

For the time being, she doesn't have a golf cart big enough to carry more than a couple of people and their luggage, so Holly has enlisted a small army of her neighbors to show up with their carts and ferry people to and from the new dock. It's a problem she'll have to solve at some point, as walking from the new dock to Main Street isn't nearly as convenient as hopping off a boat at the old dock and walking a few hundred yards up a sidewalk.

Parking at the edge of the sand, Holly gets out and surveys the dock and the water beyond. She's still the only one there, and from a distance, she can see a large boat approaching the island. The decorations for the dock are all in place: oversized plastic candy canes sticking out of the sand like guideposts; tall lights wrapped from top to bottom in tinsel; solar-powered Christmas lights lining the dock that will glow brightly at night.

Several golf carts approach on the sandy, unpaved road, and Holly waves at Buckhunter, Fiona, Cap, and Vance Guy. She still has the husbands of all three triplets coming to help, as well as Bonnie and Wyatt Bender. Between the ten of them, they should easily be able to get everyone over to the B&B in no time, and their first real group of tourists (not reality show competitors, not wedding guests— actual *tourists*) since the pirates and the fishermen will officially be amongst them.

When the boat docks, the islanders are lined up like the crew of an all-inclusive resort, ready to greet everyone and start directing the action. The first people to descend onto the dock's wooden planks are a small cluster of women who remind Holly of her mother. They're toned and tanned, with perfectly smoothed hair and wrists full of shiny bracelets. Their nails are manicured and their luggage sets all match.

"Hello, honey," one of the women says to Holly in an accent that's unmistakably Texan. "I'm Beth Fairbanks, and these are my fellow Alpha Chi Omega sisters, Henny, Astrid, and Paulina." She points at each of the other women in turn.

"Welcome to Christmas Key," Holly says. "We'll get you all to the B&B and checked in right away. Just head on over to the carts there and one of our drivers will help you with your luggage." She points at the line of carts and turns to greet the next guests.

"Holly?" A woman close to Holly's age in a blouse with a little smear of pink lipstick on her front teeth extends a hand. "Jackie, from Island Paradise Excursions."

"It's nice to finally meet you!" Holly shakes her hand warmly. She and Jackie have been talking on the phone and exchanging emails for months as they've planned for the day that the company would start bringing guests to the island, and they've finally done it. "We're really glad to have you here."

"And we're glad to be here," Jackie says, letting go of Holly's hand. "Getting this weekend together has been—" Jackie feigns a fever, putting the back of her hand to her forehead like she's broken out in a sweat. "These Alpha Chi Omegas are a demanding bunch!" she whispers confidentially, leaning in and putting a hand in front of her mouth.

"Is this whole group a sorority?" Holly watches as the women pour forth from the boat, most looking like carbon copies of Beth Fairbanks and her friends, just at different ages.

"It's a reunion, of sorts. The Alpha Chis decided to sign up for this event and I think we have ladies here from about age twenty-five to sixty-five," Jackie pauses as two women who appear to be at the upper range of this estimate pass between them, dragging wheeled luggage behind them. "And then we have our murder mystery group, but they'll come off the boat last, after everyone else has gone to check in."

"So have the women seen them yet? Do they know what the mystery is all about?" Holly waves at Wyatt and Bonnie as they load guests into their carts and start to drive towards the B&B.

"No. The whole murder mystery is still a total secret," Jackie assures her. "The performers have been hiding out, so to speak, and all of their costumes and everything are boxed up. No one knows a thing."

"Well, we're all ready on this end," Holly says. "We've got this place decked out for the holidays, and the B&B's dining room is all set for the dinner tonight."

"Perfect." Jackie moves the strap of her purse from one shoulder to the other. "As soon as these Alpha Chis are on their way, I'll introduce you to Hamlet and Margo, and they can fill you in on the event a bit more."

Holly recognizes the names as those of the husband and wife who run the murder mystery events, and she's more than a little curious to meet them. In an effort to speed things along, she starts moving luggage into the back of golf carts herself and waving people off.

As soon as the last carts have disappeared around the bend, an elderly couple appears on the deck of the boat. The woman is slightly hunched over and wearing a fur stole and pearl earrings. The man has silvery-gray hair that's slicked back from his wide forehead, and he's got a satin ascot tucked into the front of a navy blue smoking jacket.

"Hamlet and Margo?" Holly asks Jackie tentatively, though she's hoping these are just performers.

"Yep." Jackie nods her blonde head and gives a close-lipped smile. "They're real characters. You'll love them."

"Well," Holly says with a sigh. "They'll fit right in here, that's for sure."

"Older population?" Jackie raises an eyebrow.

"Our average age is seventy-two," Holly says. "Actually, better make that seventy-one and a half; we've acquired a sixteen and a twenty-three year old in the past year."

Jackie chuckles. "That's sweet. I bet it's fun to live with older people."

"Actually, it is. They're wonderful. And I'm sure Margo and Hamlet are going to be great."

"Dear me," Margo says, walking gingerly down the steps to the dock with Hamlet's shaky arm for support. "This place is just *precious*."

"Welcome, welcome," Holly says, turning the volume on her voice up a notch or two out of habit. After spending her life on Christmas Key, her enunciation and tone automatically adjust in the presence of anyone over sixty-five.

She greets Hamlet and Margo and sends them on their way with Gwen's husband, who steers them to his cart and loads their luggage onto the back with ease. Their voices carry down to the edge of the dock, where Jackie is motioning for a group of other people to come down and join them.

The woman who comes out first is gorgeous: tall, long-legged, and with a full face of make up. She carries a little handled case and wears oversized sunglasses, and appears to Holly to be a Rockette looking for seasonal work. After her comes a plump, white-haired couple who are decidedly more spry than Hamlet and Margo. The woman wears her hair in a neat topknot, and the man has a full beard and a rounded belly. They wear matching Hawaiian shirts and khaki shorts.

"This is our elf," Jackie says as the beautiful woman approaches them. "And this is Santa and Mrs. Claus."

"Hello. Welcome. How are you?" Holly says to each of the performers. "Nice to meet you, Santa," she adds, not missing a beat. "And Mrs. Claus—welcome to Christmas Key."

"This is just lovely," Mrs. Claus says breathily. "Gorgeous. And these decorations—honey, we should get something like this at the North Pole." She turns to Santa, totally in character as she touches the plastic candy canes lined up along the dock.

Holly laughs. "You guys are good."

"And this is Nigel Winters," Jackie says, resting a hand on the arm of a man wearing a matching emerald green tracksuit and gold rings on both pinkies. He looks like a bookie. "Nigel is Santa's business manager, and he's here to make sure the event goes according to plan."

"Wait..." Holly looks back and forth between the people who are standing on the dock. "Like, the business manager of the performers, or...?"

"No," Jackie says seriously, though Holly detects more than an ounce of mirth behind the twitch of her lips. "He looks after Santa Claus and makes sure everything goes according to Mr. Claus's wishes."

"Like he makes sure Santa has the right brand of beer and that there are only yellow flowers backstage on tour?" Holly jokes.

Nigel Winters looks at her like she's just said something deeply offensive. "I look after all aspects of Santa's travels and appearances."

"Okay," Holly says. "Got it. We're thrilled to have you all here."

In short order, she sorts out the cart situation and gets everyone to the B&B. The performers never break character and Holly catches herself several times as she nearly says something that indicates her disbelief in their performance. But maybe this is how it's supposed to be—maybe the only way you can pull off a real murder mystery weekend from start to finish is to fully commit to the characters, Holly thinks. Otherwise, wouldn't the whole thing end up being a tongue-in-cheek, wink-wink affair? This way, even she is allowed to buy into the drama and the intrigue.

By six o'clock, Santa and Mrs. Claus are in the dining room. Gone are the Hawaiian shirts, replaced by full holiday regalia. Santa's cheeks are rosy and his red coat is belted with a shiny black belt, its gold buckle polished until it reflects the Christmas lights that fill the dining room.

"Good evening, young lady," Mrs. Claus says. Her hands are clasped in front of her white dress, and she has a red apron tied around her waist.

"Can I get you anything before the kids show up?" Holly offers. "Egg nog? Hot cocoa?"

"No, thank you." Santa runs a hand over his white beard. "We're just fine and dandy. This is a lovely place you have here, Holly."

"And what a pretty Christmas name," Mrs. Claus adds, taking a step closer and looking Holly in the eye. "We've already heard the history of the island from the lady at the front desk, and oh my," Mrs. Claus says in a soft voice, "your grandparents sound like wonderful people."

Unexpectedly, the desire to cry chokes Holly. She normally keeps herself busy enough that she doesn't have the time to miss her grandparents, but as she looks into Mrs. Claus's warm, shining eyes, she has a moment where she really and truly just wants them both there.

The spell is broken by Mexi and Mori's excited shouts. "Santa!" they both yell, running through the open doors of the dining room. They stop short when they see the giant, decorated tree in the corner of the room (a fake tree that Holly drags out of storage every year and sets up in the dining room), and their jaws drop at the stockings hung around the room.

"Do we have stockings here?" Mexi asks, looking at the names that Holly and Bonnie have carefully added to each red and white sock. "There's Mommy," he says, "and Miss Ellen."

"I see Mr. Cap and there's Grandma!" Mori adds.

"You guys are right over there." Holly puts one hand on Mori's shoulder and points to where she's hung their stockings, closest to the overstuffed velvet chair that Santa will sit in. The boys run over and stare up at their stockings with awe.

"Seems like they've forgotten about the main event already," Santa says, laughing heartily as he pats his stomach with both white-gloved hands.

"Boys," Calista says, calling her sons over. "Do you want to come and visit with Santa?"

"No, no," Santa says, "let them have their fun. You're only young once."

But both boys come racing back just as Santa gets situated in the chair. Holly stands back and and admires the scene: the room is lit and sparkling with lights and tinsel and decorations. The tree glows brightly, and the colors of the stockings match the red linens they've draped over all of the round tables. Mexi and Mori are on their knees in front of Santa, already peeling back the plastic wrappers on the candy canes that Mrs. Claus has handed them. They're ready to listen to Santa read *The Night Before Christmas* in his booming voice, and he opens the book grandly, running his gloved finger over the words.

"*Twas the night before Christmas*," he begins.

"This is amazing," Vance Guy says, stepping up beside Holly. They take in the scene together as Calista snaps photos of the boys with Santa on her iPhone. "Thanks for setting this up for our little guys. I'm glad they get to meet Santa before he gets whacked."

Holly gives a quiet snort. "Who says Santa is getting whacked?"

Vance shrugs. "I can see it coming. I've been reading Jantzen Parks novels at night, and I'm starting to see everything as one big murder mystery plot."

"So whodunnit, detective?" Holly whispers, leaning in so that no one else hears them making cracks about Santa's potential untimely demise.

"I think Bonnie is the vixen who lures Santa out onto the water at midnight."

"Wait," Holly laughs. "Our Bonnie?"

"Yeah. I think Bonnie gets him to go out on a little rowboat with her for a glass of wine under the winter moon, and somehow Santa falls overboard. But was he pushed? Did they just drink too much and get tipsy?"

Holly shakes her head. "First Santa gets knocked off, and now Bonnie is responsible?" She gives a wry smile. "I'm glad you're channeling at least some of this vivid imagination into books of your own, Vance."

"Book. Singular," he corrects. "And I've barely touched it since the bookstore opened. Having kids and running a business takes a big toll on book progress."

"Luckily," Holly says, patting him on the shoulder, "your fans will wait. Whenever that book does come out, we'll all be here, lining up for our autographed copies."

"I got some great shots," Calista says as she walks up to Holly and Vance with the screen of her phone facing outwards to show them.

"Oooh, that one is really good." Holly points at a shot of the boys. It's from behind, and they're both on their knees by Santa's shiny black boots, looking up at him in awe as he reads to them. Santa's face is full of expression and the lights around the room make it look like a professional shot. "Would you mind if I used that one on the island's social media accounts?"

Vance and Calista look at the photo together. The boys' faces aren't visible, and the beauty of the photo is undeniable.

"Sure. Let me send it to you," Calista says, opening a text to Holly.

"Sugar!" Bonnie rushes into the dining room. Her hair is perfectly coiffed and she's wearing a shiny gold top over a pair of black dress pants. They entire island has been invited to the adults-only holiday party in the dining room, and they're ready to get everything underway just as soon as the little ones clear out.

"What's up, Bon?" Holly pulls her phone out of her back pocket as it buzzes; Calista's photo has just come through.

"Jantzen isn't feeling well."

Holly's brow furrows. "He's not? What's wrong?"

Bonnie shrugs and makes a cartoonish face of concern. "I have no idea, doll. I called his room to make sure he'd be here for the party, and he said his stomach was on the fritz. Should I send him something?"

"Why don't you take him a 7Up and some crackers from the kitchen?" Holly says, following Bonnie down the hallway and leaving the Guy family with Santa and Mrs. Claus. "On second thought, why don't I take it to him?" she says. Chances are good that if Bonnie shows up at Jantzen Parks' door, she'll invite herself in and disappear from the radar.

Bonnie gives her a sly grin. "Don't trust me, sugar?" She bumps the swinging door to the kitchen with her round backside. Iris and Jimmy Cafferkey and their small kitchen crew are already hard at work inside, plating hors d'oeuvres and polishing glasses.

"Trust you with an available, attractive man?" Holly raises an eyebrow. "Not for a second."

Iris raises an empty glass as if she's toasting to what Holly's just said. "Here, here," she says flatly.

Bonnie bats her eyes at both of them and steps around the people working in the kitchen to grab a tray and a glass for the 7Up.

"Here, let me drop this stuff off with Jantzen and then we'll get this party started," Holly says, taking the tray from Bonnie's hands as they approach Jantzen's room.

She knocks once and waits. Nothing.

"Knock again," Bonnie says in a loud whisper. She's standing to the right of the door, hands clasped together as she waits for him to open up. "Just knock harder!"

Holly shoots Bonnie a look that says "I know what I'm doing," and then raps on the door again with her fist. "Mr. Parks?" she says. "It's Holly. I heard you weren't feeling well, and I brought you something."

The night before at the Ho Ho—following Jantzen's successful reading at A Sleigh Full of Books—he'd knocked back enough rum to float a boat. He'd imbibed so much of Joe Sacamano's homemade coconut rum that he'd started singing along to the music that played over the speakers, at one point sweeping Maria Agnelli into his arms for a spin around the floor of the small bar. Everyone had laughed and Wyatt Bender bought Jantzen another round. Holly figures that this is what's behind his upset stomach, but she politely keeps that opinion to herself.

"Mr. Parks, I've got some Tums in my desk if you think that will help," Holly offers, still talking to the closed door. She knocks lightly again and this time, the door unlatches, as if someone's turned the handle. It swings open slowly and Holly takes a step back into the hallway. "Whoa," she says.

Bonnie reaches out for Holly's arm and pulls her close, nearly knocking the tray out of her hands in the process. "What in the devil's name..." she says in a hushed voice.

The room is cast in a shadow of darkness. The palm tree outside the window blocks the light from the pool deck, and as the women stand there, they can see the dark outline of a body on the floor. It isn't moving.

"Jantzen?" Bonnie calls into the room, not making a move. "Honey, are you okay?"

But when Holly finally gathers the nerve to reach in and flip on the light, and both lamps on the bedside tables come to life, they realize that it's not Jantzen Parks sprawled out on the carpet of the guest room, but Santa's gorgeous, leggy elf.

Jantzen Parks is nowhere to be found.

5

MEXI AND MORI HAVE BEEN SPIRITED AWAY FROM THE PARTY BY THE time Holly and Bonnie come rushing out into the dining room in a panic. The B&B is crawling with Alpha Chi Omegas in brightly-colored dresses and gallons of hairspray and perfume, and the islanders are streaming into the dining room dressed for a holiday cocktail party.

Holly's first instinct is to find Fiona and get help for the girl on the floor, but as soon as she sees the crowd, she remembers: everything is fair game for the murder mystery. As she stops short, Bonnie bumps into her from behind.

"Sugar," she says breathlessly. "We need to get help for that poor girl. We need Fiona."

"Wait," Holly says, holding up a hand. "What if this is all part of the game?"

"Ohhhh, the game," Bonnie says. "So that means Jantzen Parks might not have killed her?"

"I don't think she's really dead at all, Bon."

Just then, Hamlet and Margo walk into the dining room. Margo's hand is looped through the tuxedoed arm of her elderly husband, her lips heavily lipsticked and puckered as she assesses the room. Holly waves at them.

"Just the people I was looking for," Holly says breathlessly, rushing over to them. "I went to take something to Jantzen Parks, and I found Santa's elf on the floor of his room."

Margo sucks in a sharp breath. "Oh my," she says, putting one shaky hand to her chest. Her knuckles are knobbed and she wears loose gold rings on several fingers. "We better get the doctor. What are you waiting for?"

"I thought...I just assumed...isn't this part of the game?" Holly asks, puzzled.

Margo looks at Hamlet and they both shrug. "Guess you won't know until you get that doctor," Hamlet says, glancing around the room with a hint of mischief in his eyes.

Ah, so it is part of the game! Holly thinks. She immediately kicks into high gear, knowing that her reaction to this first part of the mystery is integral to getting the ball rolling.

"Fiona!" Holly shouts, spinning wildly. "Has anyone seen Dr. Potts?"

Maria Agnelli is standing in the middle of the dining room with Jake and Katelynn, and she puts a hand to her mouth. "Is everything okay? Has there been a murder?"

"I'm not sure," Holly says, walking up to them and putting a hand on Mrs. Agnelli's birdlike upper arm. "I just need Fiona."

"I saw her out on the sidewalk a few minutes ago," Jake says, pointing his thumb over his shoulder to indicate Main Street behind them.

Holly rushes through the French doors and takes the few steps through her small lobby and out onto the front steps of the B&B.

"Fee!" she calls, spotting her best friend on the other side of Main Street talking to Millie Bradford as she locks up the salon inside of Poinsettia Plaza. "Fee, we need you!"

There must be something to the pitch and tone of Holly's voice that indicates seriousness, because Fiona stops talking mid-sentence and dashes across the street in her black suede pants and black, sleeveless turtleneck top. Holly has told her to dress for a holiday party, and she's gone all out, even polishing her fingers and toes red and strapping on a pair of sparkly flat sandals.

"What is it?" Fiona asks, putting both of her hands on Holly's shoulders. "What's going on?"

"There's someone passed out on the floor of Jantzen's room," Holly says. Without having really put forth any exertion, she's nearly out of breath. "I don't know her name—it's the elf who came in on the boat today."

Fiona brushes past Holly and hurries through the lobby and down the hallway. "Which room?" she calls over her shoulder. But she really doesn't need to ask, as a small crowd has already gathered outside of the Coconut Grove suite. "Excuse me," Fiona says, gently moving two Alpha Chi Omegas out of the way and stepping around Cap Duncan and two of the triplets, who are hanging onto each other in shock.

"I need everyone to clear the room," Fiona says, standing between the unmoving body and the onlookers. "Holly, can you stay and help me?" She falls to her knees and turns her back to the crowd.

Holly automatically kicks into mayor-mode, sweeping her hands and forcing everyone away from the door. "You heard Dr. Potts," she says brusquely. "Let's give her space. You'll know what's going on as soon as we know."

Holly closes the door to the guest room and stands there, hands over her mouth as she watches Fiona attend to the woman.

"We've got a little work ahead of us," Fiona says, taking the woman's hands in hers. "Up you go," she says, taking a deep breath and holding it as the woman opens her eyes and lets Fiona pull her to a standing position.

Holly's hands fall from her face. "So she's totally fine?"

"Shhhh," Fiona says, waving her hands wildly to quiet Holly. "There are ears all up and down that hallway out there."

Holly glances at the closed door.

"Listen, I have to know what's going to happen so that I don't actually start administering medical attention to people who are just acting, so I knew about this," Fiona explains in a loud whisper.

"You did?"

"Yeah, and Jake does, too. We had to know whether real crimes and real medical emergencies were happening. And now that you're here, I think it would behoove you to know what's happening, too."

"No!" Holly nearly shouts, holding up her hands like a shield. "I want to be surprised. I want to play the game!"

"Hol," Fiona says, watching the formerly fallen elf fluff out her hair and touch up her lipstick in the mirror over the dresser. "You're the mayor. It would really help us if you were on board with every step of this game."

"You should really hear it all," the elf says, turning to them as she puts the lid back on her lipstick tube and drops it into her purse. "It's pretty fun. The last time we did it, some old guy tried to give me mouth-to-mouth." She puckers up her face to show them how gross this was for her. "And now that I'm 'dead,' I need to disappear."

"Disappear?" Holly looks back at Fiona.

"Right. That's our next step."

As if on cue, there is a light tap on the window of the guest room. Holly walks over and sees Jake's face peering in at them. He motions for her to open the window, and she unlocks it and pushes it open. Jake is standing on the pool deck, covered by the fronds of the short palm tree that blocks the window from the pool.

"Hey," he says. "Is she ready?"

"I'm always ready," the elf says with one lifted brow. "A good actress has to stay on her toes."

Holly watches as the elf slings her purse across her body like a messenger bag and reaches one long leg through the open window. She lets Jake grab her around the waist and guide her out into the darkening night. "See ya," the elf says with a small wave. She and Jake disappear from view.

"What the hell?" Holly spins and looks at Fiona. "How are we going to explain that a body went missing? And where is she going?"

"We've got this all covered. Just follow my lead."

In short order, Fiona wheels a stretcher over from her office inside Poinsettia Plaza, Jake returns to help her "lift the body," and she pushes a stretcher of pillows covered by a sheet through a crowd of gobsmacked guests in the B&B's dining room. Holly tries to gauge the believability of the act, and on some faces she sees real shock (possibly the residual drama of actually seeing Ray Bradford wheeled away from the island on a stretcher, or little Mori Guy being pushed across the street to Fiona's office after falling into the B&B's pool in the spring), and on others—mostly the Alpha Chi Omegas—she sees excitement as the wheels begin to turn and the guests start to sleuth.

"Jake," Holly says, pulling him firmly by the arm once the guests are all gathered in the B&B awaiting the final word on the elf and on the whereabouts of the suddenly missing Jantzen Parks. "You knew about this?"

Jake shrugs. "I don't care if I win the award for best amateur detective," he says, smiling at her. "I know you like to win, but I'm fine just helping the game along."

"Well, I'm roped into it now," she says, leaning close so that no one else around them will hear. "So tell me—where is the elf? And where is Jantzen?"

"The elf is in the 'safe house' for the weekend—the empty bungalow on White Christmas Way. Anyone who gets murdered or needs to be hidden for the weekend will go there. And her name is Molly."

"You're on a first name basis with the dead elf?" Holly wrinkles her nose. "Cute. But who else is going to get murdered?"

Christmas music is playing on the speakers throughout the dining room and people are drinking wine and champagne in goblets and flutes, talking and laughing over the hors d'oeuvres that line the buffet table along one wall. Several of the Alpha Chi Omegas are wearing hot pink, and a number of them appear to have been drinking all afternoon in anticipation of the evening's big event, if the amount of tinsel wrapped around necks and wound into makeshift tiaras is any indication.

"You'll just have to wait and—" Jake is about to tease Holly and drag out the suspense a little when a high-pitched scream fills the dining room.

"Santa!" Mrs. Claus wails, crumbling to the ground next to her husband as his body falls to the carpet.

Everyone goes silent. The small Christmas tree next to Santa's big chair topples to the ground like a delayed reaction to Santa's fall, ornaments crashing into one another and shattering on impact.

As the crowd absorbs the fact that not only is there a dead elf cooling across the street in Fiona's medical office, but a potentially dead Santa in their midst, a real wave of shock ripples through the room.

They all stare at his body and watch Mrs. Claus running her hand through his white hair as she wails. The only sound in the room is the smooth voice of Bing Crosby on the speakers.

6

"What in the name of Sam Hill?" Wyatt Bender says. He puts an arm around Bonnie's shoulders as they stand on the street in front of the B&B.

Once again, Fiona has cleared the room and gotten a tired-looking Jake to help her with the crime scene and the moving of the body. Holly has her arms folded across her chest as she looks at the faces of her neighbors and listens to the excited chatter of the Alpha Chi Omegas. She's quickly gathered that this isn't their first murder mystery weekend, and from the darting glances and whispered guesses, she can tell that they're already hard at work trying to fit the pieces of the puzzle together.

"I wonder what happened to Jantzen Parks?" Katelynn says loudly. Her eyes pick through the crowd, but Jantzen is still nowhere to be seen.

"He stopped by the gift shop this afternoon," Gwen says, turning to her identical sisters, Gen and Glen. They nod at one another in confirmation.

"In fact," Gen adds, "he asked whether we had any sort of over the counter sleeping pills."

"And then," Glen jumps in, "he told me he might need a jug of water, some granola bars, and sunscreen."

A ripple of discussion races through the crowd.

"Did he ask about getting off the island?" an Omega with a swingy red ponytail and an abundance of freckles asks with an intense frown.

"That was me he asked," Cap says, raising one hand. "He dropped by the cigar shop earlier and had some questions about boats and tides and how far we were from Key West or the Dry Tortugas."

Holly leans into Bonnie and bumps her shoulder. "Hey," she whispers. "This is pretty fun."

"I don't know, sugar," Bonnie says. Holly can feel an actual shiver run over her friend. "I'm kind of worried about Santa."

"He looked a little worse for wear in there," Wyatt says, leaning around Bonnie to look Holly in the eye. "And Mrs. Claus seemed genuinely concerned."

Bonnie nods in agreement. "What if he really had a heart attack? Like Ray?"

Holly glances around quickly to make sure Millie Bradford isn't within earshot. She doesn't want to open up the fresh wound and have people start talking about Ray's heart attack and sudden passing during one of their village council meetings this past spring.

"You guys," Holly says quietly, "this is all part of the game. It has to be—think about it: two dead bodies within a half an hour of each other? Come on."

Wyatt pulls Bonnie closer to him and gives Holly a wink to let her know that he agrees with her, but is taking the opportunity to comfort Bonnie for all it's worth. *That sly devil*, Holly thinks.

"Okay, everyone," Jake says. He's standing on the top step of the B&B with a serious look on his face. "This evening has taken a grim turn."

Hamlet moves through the crowd with one knobby hand raised in the air. "Let's all regroup," he says over the rising chatter. "We've got a real situation on our hands here. Molly, our beloved elf, has passed away under mysterious circumstances. And now Santa..." He shakes his head and reaches for Margo, who has appeared at her husband's side. They hold hands and look at one another. "Well, there really aren't any good words, are there?"

"No, dear." Margo looks sad. "No good words."

"What we're going to need now is for everyone to pull together and help us figure out what's going on here." Hamlet searches the crowd. "Who can help us lead that charge?"

"That would be me, sir," Jake says, stepping forward. "I'm the island's only police officer, and I've been present for both incidents. I'd be happy to take charge of the investigation."

"Thank you, Officer." Margo puts a shaky hand on Jake's muscled arm and lets it linger there a moment longer than is necessary.

"Okay," Jake says, clapping both hands together and rubbing them like he's sitting before a Thanksgiving feast. "We have one Christmas elf, a Miss—" Jake pulls a small spiral notepad from his back pocket and flips it open. "Miss Molly Tucker from Pennsylvania. Aged twenty-four. Molly was found unresponsive this evening in the Coconut Grove suite. All of her personal items were accounted for, and the last person she was seen with was a Mr. Jantzen Parks, who was staying in the Coconut Grove suite."

"Any signs of a struggle? Knife wounds? Ligature marks?" One of the Omegas asks loudly, putting a hand in the air like she's in school.

"Definite signs of a struggle," Jake says, nodding. He consults his spiral notebook again. "Miss Tucker had very recently passed when we found her."

"Drugs!" a woman near Holly whispers. "It has to be drugs," she says knowingly to her friend, her mouth a thin line as she nods.

"Could we access the scene of the crime?" Hamlet prompts Jake.

"Well, we hesitate to call it a crime scene just yet," Jake says. "So far we're treating this as an unfortunate passing. But we have preserved the room as it was, and we can bring people through in groups of three or four to see if any clues remain. But I have to warn you," Jake adds, "you cannot touch anything."

"What about Santa?" Miguel pipes up. "He didn't look so good."

"Santa is another story," Jake says. As if on cue, Fiona steps out of

Poinsettia Plaza and walks across the street with her head hanging low. Both of her hands are shoved into the pockets of the cargo pants she's wearing under her white lab coat. "Dr. Potts is here now, so let's see what she has to say."

"Hi, everyone," Fiona says. She walks up the B&B steps and stands next to Jake. "I'm afraid we couldn't save him." Fiona looks at everyone with sad eyes. "I did my best. It was sudden and unexpected, and that's all I can say right now."

"Wait!" Someone shouts from the crowd. It's Jimmy Cafferkey. "I saw Santa at the pool earlier this afternoon when he first checked in. He was holding a glass of whiskey in one hand, a cigar in the other, and was eating a burger from Jack Frosty's."

"Do you think it was a heart attack?" Maggie Sutter asks. "Sounds like he was doing a real number on the old ticker there."

"I've looked for all the typical signs of heart attack, and I'm just not sure in this case," Fiona says. She looks up at Jake. "There are some things I'm concerned with, but I need to do a bit more investigating."

"Can we see the dining room, too?" Miguel asks over the sound of people chattering once again.

"Of course. The dining room is less of an issue because we were all in there already and saw the whole thing happen. We can go in there right now and everyone can have a look around," Jake says. He steps aside so that people can stampede past him and get back into the B&B to start piecing things together.

"Did you get a role in this game?" Holly asks Miguel as people rush past them to head back inside. "I feel like you're our Chief Inquisitor or something."

"I like the sound of that," Miguel says. His hair is still damp from a quick shower, and he's clean-shaven. "But I just got a paper that said 'concerned citizen—ask a lot of questions' and I don't want to fall down on the job."

"So far so good," Holly says, giving him a thumbs-up.

"Hey, thanks for hanging out with me at the Ho Ho last night."

"I had a good time," Holly says. She and Miguel had gone over after Jantzen's reading at A Sleigh Full of Books and shut the place down with Bonnie, Wyatt, Katelynn, and Jake. They'd laughed and danced until well after one o'clock. "I'm not sure I can stay out that late every night, but it was fun."

"Bonnie is hilarious," Miguel says. "Are she and Wyatt a thing?"

"You'd think so, wouldn't you?" Holly looks over at them; Wyatt's arm is still around Bonnie's shoulders. "They've been dancing in circles around each other for a couple of years now, so we'll see."

There's a slight pause between them. Holly scans Miguel's face. Having someone else on the island close to her own age has been refreshing, and watching him find his footing on Christmas Key and get to know everyone has reconfirmed to Holly once again what a special place her little island is.

"Should we go and see whether we can crack this case?" Miguel asks, putting out his elbow like he's offering it to Holly. She looks at it and then slips her hand through the crook of his arm.

"Oh, definitely. I'm ready to super-sleuth my way to some answers here. I wanna know whodunnit."

"Then let's go figure it out."

She and Miguel take the steps together and walk into the dining room arm-in-arm.

By midnight the dining room looks like a gym after a particularly rowdy prom. Holly is exhausted, but the last of the guests have drifted to their rooms, leaving little bits of tinsel everywhere and plates of half-eaten hors d'oeuvres and empty glasses on the tables. The sound system is still quietly playing Christmas carols, and there are chairs scattered all over the room.

"This is a mess," Holly says. "And it has to be ready for breakfast in seven hours."

"This room looks like it's been through three wars and a goat roping," Bonnie adds, her fists on both hips as she assesses the damage.

"We've got this." Miguel is still with them, and without hesitation, he starts gathering and moving chairs back to the tables. "I'll do all the rearranging if you ladies want to bus tables and get organized for breakfast."

Holly feels a wave of relief wash over her as Miguel moves three and four chairs at a time as compared to the one or two that she and Bonnie can drag across the room in one go. "Thank you, Miguel," she says. "Bon, you grab the dirty tablecloths and I'll start collecting dishes."

"Hey, I'm here to help," Fiona says, walking into the dining room. "I saw this place when we all walked out and realized that it wasn't going to clean itself."

"You guys are lifesavers," Holly says. "I really should pay you more."

"Are you going to be flush enough with cash after this weekend to start paying us what we're worth?" Fiona teases.

Holly pretends to mentally calculate a dollar figure as she scrapes cheese and fruit onto an empty platter and stacks the small hors d'oeuvres plates on a table. "Ummm, no," she finally says. "Not quite. But I can pay you in coconuts and undying affection if you want."

"Works for me," Bonnie says. She's got an armful of red tablecloths shot through with gold thread and she's on her way to the laundry room to start a load. "Should we do white linens for breakfast?"

"I think those are ironed and hanging in the laundry room," Holly calls after her.

"You really do run this all yourself, don't you?" Miguel is busy putting eight chairs around each round table, counting them off to make sure he's getting it right.

"Well, not really," Holly admits. "Without Bonnie I'd get nothing done, and honestly, everyone on this island pitches in and makes it happen. If I didn't have all the free labor, I'd be dead in the water."

"Maybe go easy on the 'dead' jokes," Fiona says. "You know, since we have a dead elf and a dead Santa on our hands."

Holly laughs. "True. Very true."

"What do you make of all this?" Miguel asks as he passes by Holly with four chairs stacked in his arms. The veins and muscles flex on his arms as he sets the chairs down and separates them.

"The murder mystery?" Holly lifts a heavy tray with effort, balancing it in her arms so that no glasses or plates slide off.

"Yeah. These people are completely on board. Like they're buying into it 100%."

"I think that's the whole idea," Fiona says. She's been gathering the tinsel from the dining room floor and has dragged a vacuum out of a closet to get everything as clean as possible.

"It seems fun," Miguel says. "But it's hard for me to completely buy into the fact that two people are dead, and I'm not quite sure how anyone else believes it, either."

"Well, they aren't *really* dead," Holly says. "So yeah, I can see how it would be hard to completely suspend your disbelief."

Bonnie walks back into the room with a stack of ironed white tablecloths draped over one arm. "That's real life though, isn't it, sugar?" she asks, jumping right into their conversation. "In pretty much everything, you've got to suspend your disbelief a little bit."

Miguel frowns. "How so?"

"What are you, honey? Twenty-five?" Bonnie unfolds the first tablecloth and lets it settle over one of the rounds. "And I'm not saying that in a patronizing way."

"I'm twenty-three," Miguel says. He stops what he's doing and looks at Bonnie.

"Okay. Then maybe you haven't quite realized it yet, but life is full of things that feel...unreal. And some things are. But even the most real things out there require you to put aside what you might really think and feel and just sort through it. Let your head and your heart do the work whether you believe something is really happening or not."

"Examples?" Miguel asks with curiosity.

Bonnie stops and puts both hands on the back of a chair. She levels her gaze at him. "Examples. Well. My husband had a heart attack in the middle of a Publix and left me a widow one day when I least expected it. That really happened, as many things do. But for a while, I had to let myself believe that it hadn't. Just to get up in the morning, I had to give my mind and my heart permission to think that maybe he was just away for work and would be coming back home to me. You see what I'm saying?"

"Kind of," Miguel admits.

"It's a way of coping. Letting yourself choose to believe or disbelieve. These people are here for who knows what reasons. Maybe one of the women is a new widow and she needs to believe in something else for a weekend. Maybe another is a lawyer who puts in eighty-hour workweeks and she needs to let herself believe there's something else in the universe besides laws and courtrooms and long nights of research and preparation. Who knows."

"Good points," Miguel agrees.

"So if someone wants to believe for a few days that Santa and one of his elves died mysterious deaths on a tropical island, I say let 'em. And if it heightens the mystery to think that some famous author has anything to do with it, then I'll play along. I'll let my head and heart believe anything for a minute—especially if it makes life more fun."

"Yeah," Holly says in a teasing tone, hoping to lighten the mood. "And let's not even talk about how Bonnie suspended her disbelief for a weekend and boarded a pirate ship with a guy wearing an eyepatch and breeches."

"Wait, what?" Miguel laughs.

Bonnie wads up a used linen napkin and tosses it in Holly's direction. "Yeah, let's not talk about that," she says, shooting her friend a warning look.

"So what's next?" Fiona asks as she plugs in the vacuum and pulls the cord out as far as it will go. "Do we start guessing who the murderer is? Or why we've got two bodies on our hands?"

"Yeah," Holly says. "I think we start sleuthing. Don't you have the answers, Fee?"

"Me?" Fiona puts her foot on the button to turn on the vacuum. "No. All I was told to do was clear the scenes, remove the bodies, so to speak, and then declare them both deceased. My job is done unless people ask for some of the details of the deaths, which I have. Beyond that, I'm as much in the dark as you all."

Holly feels a sense of excitement as she thinks back over the evening. Bonnie is right: rather than just run this mystery weekend from behind the scenes, she can jump in the game and have some fun if she wants to. And she actually really wants to.

"Should we team up and pool our resources?" she asks Fiona, Bonnie, and Miguel.

"Kind of like people forming an alliance on 'Survivor'?" Miguel offers.

"Yeah—like that. If any of us get any clues or have any ideas, we can share them and try to find the answer together."

"Good idea, Hol," Fiona agrees. She slides her phone out of her back pocket and looks at them. "I'll start a group chat with the four of us, and whenever we stumble on anything, we'll discuss."

"Got it," Bonnie says. "Now let's get this room whipped into shape so we can get some shut-eye. This old gal is exhausted."

"And ready to meet Jantzen Parks for a nightcap?" Holly guesses.

"Shhhh, sugar. Hush now and bus these tables, will you?" Bonnie gives her a wink and goes back to shaking out clean tablecloths. "Just suspend your disbelief a little, and imagine that Bonnie Lou Lane doesn't have the feminine wiles to set up a midnight date with a famous author, okay?"

With a laugh, Fiona taps the power button on the vacuum and fills the dining room with noise.

7

"CAN I OFFER YOU A SEAT BY THE WINDOW?" MARIA AGNELLI IS holding a stack of menus in her hands as she greets people at the open doorway of Jack Frosty's.

"We'd like a table anywhere," Holly says, eyeing the jukebox. "Be right there," she says to Fiona and Bonnie, hand already fishing around in the pocket of her white denim shorts.

As her friends follow Mrs. Agnelli, she skims the list of songs that she already knows like the back of her hand, then punches the button for Bruce Springsteen's "Santa Claus is Comin' to Town."

"Of course," Buckhunter says loudly, glancing over one shoulder at her as he mixes a pitcher of sweet iced tea with a long wooden spoon. "I should have known."

"Hey, I only play this one in December," she shouts back with a smile. Buckhunter shakes his head and she can tell he's forgiven her for foisting Mrs. Agnelli on him as a de facto restaurant hostess for the duration of the murder mystery weekend.

"And then," Mrs. Agnelli is saying to Fiona and Bonnie as Holly approaches their table, "she tells the other gals that she spent the night with Jantzen Parks, which means he didn't actually leave the island."

"What's happening?" Holly pulls out a chair and sits down.

"One of these island visitors was telling her friends over lunch that she had Jantzen Parks in her room last night," Fiona says with an amused half-smile.

"That's not possible," Bonnie huffs. She puts one hand to the back of her perfectly styled red hair and pats it gently. "Simply not possible."

"And why is that?" Holly goads her. She puts out a hand to take a menu from Mrs. Agnelli.

"I just don't think it's true," Bonnie says, batting her eyes. "Mr. Parks doesn't seem like the kind of man to shack up with just any old woman."

"Oh, she wasn't old," Mrs. Agnelli adds, putting one hand on the back of Fiona's chair and the other on her bony hip. "She was young and perky and blonde."

A flame of pink creeps up Bonnie's neck and she picks up her menu to fan herself. "Well," she says, "I still think it's hogwash, Maria. Now will you be a dear and bring me a sweet tea?"

Mrs. Agnelli makes a face. "I'm not a waitress, Bonnie. I'm just here to seat you and eavesdrop on all the murder talk." And with that, she turns and walks away.

"I guess you got told," Holly says with a laugh. She glances at the menu, even though it never changes and she pretty much always orders the same thing.

"So, how is it that we know what Mr. Parks was up to last night?" Fiona asks. "Huh, Bon?"

"Ladies, a woman never kisses and tells." Bonnie looks at her own menu primly. "I'm just saying that I have a strong hunch."

"So, what are we having?" Buckhunter is at the table with three tall iced teas in his hands, already anticipating their orders. "Sweet tea for my lovely bride and Miss Bonnie Lou, and an Arnold Palmer for my niece, who's saddled me with Grandma Moses as a hostess for the weekend."

"Hey, if Grandma Moses can pick up painting in her seventies,

Mrs. Agnelli can start hostessing in her eighties," Holly offers help-fully. "You might thank me later."

Buckhunter lowers his chin and stares at her. "Yeah. I might. I might also get drafted into the NBA in my fifties."

"Cheeseburger with bacon and barbecue sauce and fries for me, please," Holly says with a sweet smile, handing over her menu.

"Nachos for me, honey." Fiona holds out her menu to her husband.

"And I'll take a salad with the dressing on the side, please," Bonnie says. "Unlike these girls, I have to watch my figure."

Wisely, Buckhunter says nothing but takes their menus and disappears.

"So, what have we got?" Bonnie leans across the table conspirato-rially. "Do you think the killer is amongst us?"

The three women casually pick up their drinks and sip through straws as their eyes dart around the restaurant. Normally, Jack Frosty's wouldn't be packed, but with the influx of visitors, the joint is jumping. Nearly every table is filled by women with expensive purses resting near their pedicured, sandaled feet, and Buckhunter is moving around like a man on fire, dropping off drinks, taking orders on his notepad, and shouting at Maria Agnelli to keep her hands away from the grill.

"I was just going to put a burger on for Cap," Mrs. Agnelli shouts back.

"Well, don't!" Buckhunter shakes his head and continues to take the order for the table he's currently attending to.

Holly turns her attention back to Bonnie and Fiona. "I think the killer is..." She lets her eyes drift up to the ceiling fan above them as she ponders the scenes of the night before. "I think it's the last person we'd ever suspect."

"Duh." Fiona is unimpressed by this conclusion.

"No, really. I think there's going to be a story behind it and we're all going to be completely surprised."

"There's always a story," Bonnie says. "For instance, what do you think of that lady over there?" She tips her head ever so slightly in the direction of a brunette with a fair amount of facial work in her past. Her forehead is smooth, her lips plump, her eyes wide and curious. She can't be much shy of sixty. "What's her story?"

"With regards to the murder?" Holly asks, putting her straw to her lips.

"No, just in general."

"I think she's got money."

"Rich husband?" Bonnie asks.

"No," Holly says firmly. "She was once a world-famous model, but a drug habit sidelined her."

"A drug habit?" Fiona chokes on her iced tea. "Why drugs?"

"Because she was a top model. You know, lots of drugs in that scene." Holly waves away the question. "Anyway, she had a business manager who invested her money wisely—"

"In what?" Bonnie pulls a napkin from the dispenser at the center of the table.

"In stocks. Apple and Starbucks."

"That would have been wise," Fiona agrees, jabbing her straw into her drink to break up the ice.

"And once she hit the ten-year sober mark, she was given access to her money again."

"Which she chose to spend on plastic surgery, right?" Bonnie shoots another look in the woman's direction.

"Just a few nips and tucks. I mean, imagine being one of the most beautiful women in the world and then aging. It can't be easy."

"It's not easy even if you *aren't* a supermodel," Bonnie agrees.

"Lunch is served," Buckhunter says, swooping by and dropping off their plates. He's gone again before any of them can ask for drink refills or even say thank you.

"But is she capable of murder?" Fiona asks, pulling a cheesy nacho from the pile of food on her plate and biting the chip in half with a loud crunch.

"I once heard it said that everyone is capable of murder," Bonnie says. She spears a chunk of tomato with her fork and holds it aloft. "But most people would never go through with it."

Holly shivers unwittingly. "This is cheerful lunch talk."

Bonnie shrugs and pops the tomato into her mouth. "You're the one who wanted to bring a murder mystery to the island."

Before Holly can comment on this, Logan Pillory comes bounding up the stairs of the open air restaurant. His eyes land on Holly and he crosses the weathered wood floor in five long steps.

"Holly," he says. "I have an idea."

"Logan." Holly sets the burger she's about to bite into back onto her plate and looks up at him. "Okay, have a seat."

Before she's even done offering, he pulls out the chair and sits down in the only empty seat at the table.

"What's up, doll?" Bonnie looks at him with mild concern.

"Oh, nothing bad, Mrs. Lane," Logan says. "I just thought of something I want to do, and I was hoping Holly would help me talk my mom into it. Or approve of it. You know, if she needs to. As mayor," he adds, making a deferential nod at Holly to indicate that he knows how things work on the island.

"What's your idea?" Holly picks up a french fry and nibbles at it while she waits.

"Okay." Logan leans forward, legs splayed, face full of anticipation. "I want to start a radio station on the island."

"A radio station?" Holly's eyebrows shoot up. "Here?"

"Yeah, I've been researching it and I want to run it myself. WXMS, broadcasting live from Christmas Key."

"Wow." Holly drops her half-eaten fry. "Are you serious? A radio station on the island?"

"I love music," Logan says, nodding earnestly. "And I think it would be cool. I can get credit for it, too," he adds, referring to his predominantly online high school education, overseen by his mother.

"Well, that sounds like something worth exploring," Holly says. "I used to hang out with your great-grandpa, as a matter of fact, and we'd try to pick up signals from stations on the mainland with his shortwave radio."

"Really?" Logan's eyes widen. "That's so cool."

"Yeah, it was." Holly nods and pushes her plate towards Logan, motioning that he should eat some of her fries. He takes one. "Your great-grandma was my main teacher all through school, and when we were done with our lessons and she'd excused me for the day, your great-grandpa would let me tune into college radio stations and listen to all the music I wanted to. I'm pretty sure that's why my taste in music is so good now." She gives her hair a little toss and makes a faux self-congratulatory face. "I'm kidding. But honestly, I got really into some bands that I still love today. Radio is great."

"So you think it's a good idea?" Logan takes another fry.

"I think it's worth talking about. One hundred percent." Holly picks up another fry. "Have you pitched it to your mom yet?"

"No, I wanted to see if it was even a possibility first."

"Gotcha. Okay, let's talk to her and see what she thinks, huh?" Holly finally picks up her burger and takes a big bite.

"Thanks, Holly. I really want this to happen. I promise you, it'll be amazing."

"I don't doubt it for a minute," Holly says. "I'm around all weekend doing murder mystery stuff, so we can chat anytime she's available."

Logan stands up and pushes in his chair. "Cool. I'll see you later." He starts to leave. "Oh," he adds, turning back to the table. "Sorry to interrupt your lunch."

"No worries, kiddo," Fiona says, giving him a wave. "You've got a good idea here."

With a final wave, Logan is back down the stairs and onto Main Street, excitement and purpose in his stride.

Holly is about to comment on the notion of WXMS operating on the island when a loud crash and the sound of shattering glass makes every patron in Jack Frosty's jump.

"What the—?" Bonnie's hand flies to her mouth.

Standing at the top of the stairs is Idora Blaine-Guy. She's looking at Mrs. Agnelli as Maria looks at the shards of glass from the fallen tray she's knocked off the bar.

"Excuse me," Idora says haughtily, straitening her striped tunic and brushing off one shoulder like she's just been hit with a powdery snowball by a naughty child. "I didn't see you standing there."

"Like hell you didn't, Idora," Mrs. Agnelli crows. "You've had it in for me ever since I called you out on the fact that you're nothing but a trollop and a harlot who has her eyes on every man on this island."

Idora sucks in a breath. "Maria Agnelli," she says. "I have no designs on the men on this island." She lifts her chin. "I have been in a relationship for nearly twenty years now, and I don't intend to change that."

Mrs. Agnelli gives a sharp laugh. "Where is this imaginary boyfriend?" She ignores the broken glass and the fallen tray.

"There isn't one." Idora stares her down as she weighs the situation before continuing. "Her name is Denise and she's a nurse in Toronto." A smattering of discussion works its way through the restaurant.

"Oh, lordy, lordy," Bonnie says. Her eyes are wide.

"I guess my lunch will have to wait," Holly says under her breath, standing up. "Let me take this show off center stage and do some damage control."

Fiona nods and bites into another chip. "Good luck. I'm going to eat some of your fries before they get cold, okay?"

Holly is already halfway across the restaurant. "They're all yours," she says. "Enjoy."

"Okay," Margo says to the small crowd that's gathered in front of Mistletoe Morning Brew that evening. "We're about to embark on a scavenger hunt here that will hopefully let us explore the island a bit and maybe gather some clues."

Holly and Miguel are standing at the back of the group, each holding a peppermint mocha from the coffee shop, which has stayed open late in order to host an afternoon game of Clue for those not participating in the scavenger hunt. The sky is darkening just a shade or two, Christmas lights all up and down Main Street are on, and the air has the slightly cooler, slightly less humid feel that for Holly always means winter.

"Are Bonnie and Fiona coming?" Miguel asks. He takes a sip of his coffee.

"Fiona is helping Buckhunter at Jack Frosty's this evening. He told Mrs. Agnelli to take the night off after the big brouhaha this afternoon with her and Idora."

Miguel nearly chokes on his coffee. "I heard about that!"

"Welcome to Christmas Key, where news travels faster than most of the locals." Holly makes a face, but it's clear that not only is she used to the way gossip tears across the island, she's amused by her neighbors and their antics.

"My aunt Cristina is married to a woman. It's no big deal to me," Miguel says.

"Yeah, Ellen and Carrie-Anne have been together for years," Holly says, nodding at the coffee shop and at the two women inside as they bustle around together, cleaning up and closing down for the evening. "No one around here even gives it a second thought. I think it was just something that Idora hadn't planned on sharing. At least not like that."

"We'll be getting into teams of two to four," Margo says, passing out lists of items as she moves through the group. "And once you've found everything on your list, we'll meet at The Ho Ho Hideaway for a beer or whatever beverage tickles your fancy."

Holly holds out a hand and takes the sheet that Margo offers. She scans the items. "Is this even fair for me to participate?" she whispers to Miguel. "I know where to find every one of these things without even searching."

Miguel takes the list from her and reads the items off. "A signed copy of Jantzen Parks' new book. A photo of the island's only full-time feathered resident. Two leaves from a Palmetto Palm. An Oliva shell. A whole Sand Dollar."

"The west side of the island is covered in Oliva shells," Holly says confidentially. "The beach by my house is perfect to find any shells we need and probably the palm leaves, too."

"You're right," Miguel agrees. "This might not be fair. I still want to play though, don't you?"

Holly nods and takes a sip of her own coffee.

"Then why don't we do the scavenger hunt, but I'll find everything and you just do the driving."

"Good idea."

But clearly Margo has overheard this exchange. "And no driving!" she says, wagging a finger at them. "That would be an unfair advantage, since not all of us have golf carts."

"True," Holly acquiesces. "But we've still got this licked, even on foot."

"Ready? Everyone have a partner or a team?" Margo asks, looking around at the groups of scavenger hunters. People nod at her and women link arms excitedly like middle schoolers who've just confirmed their partners for a science project. "Okay, you've got one hour to get as many items as you can." Margo looks at her watch. "Anddddd, go!"

People scatter in all directions, and Holly and Miguel start to walk up Main Street at a leisurely pace in the direction of Cinnamon Lane.

"Excuse me!" A woman brushes past them, nearly elbowing Holly and spilling her coffee. "Sorry!"

"No worries," Holly says, watching as people consult their lists of items and disappear into shops and split off onto either Ivy Lane or Holly Lane. No one takes Cinnamon, directly ahead of them, as it's a heavily wooded path that barely registers as a street. Holly's grandparents had wanted it this way when they'd first developed the island, hoping to keep the property at the end of Cinnamon Lane shrouded in privacy for their own family.

"We can find pretty much all of that at or around my house," Holly says, pointing at the unpaved road ahead of them. "Even Marco, most likely." Marco, the island's colorful parrot, is undoubtedly the feathered resident they need to photograph, and Holly knows for a fact that he's probably perched in the Gumbo Limbo tree in her front yard, just as he was when she left the house that day.

They take Cinnamon Lane casually, still drinking their coffees.

Miguel rolls up the list of items and sticks it in the back pocket of his shorts like the baton that relay runners might pass to each other in a race.

"So, overall," Holly says, "how are you feeling? Settled in here? I know the homesickness comes and goes."

"Like I said, everyone here is really nice. It's just hard to assimilate. And to be the only person in their twenties," he adds. "Although I know you and Emily Cafferkey are barely in your thirties."

Holly tips her head in acknowledgment of this fact. "I know how you feel. Growing up, Emily and I really only had each other, and when Jake moved here I think I jumped on him and nearly suffocated him because I was so happy to see someone else my age."

Miguel gives a little laugh that he muffles with his coffee cup, which he brings to his lips.

"What?" Holly feels a flush creep over her face.

"Nothing," Miguel says. "I heard you and Jake had a thing, and just the way you described it—that you jumped on him—it was kind of funny."

"I guess I should have expected that you would have heard about me and Jake. You know, given the fact that no one around here can keep anything to themselves."

"I heard about River, too."

"What?" This actually stops Holly in her tracks.

"I was replacing a few light bulbs in the B&B one day, and Maggie Sutter cornered me while I was up on a ladder. She told me all about it: baseball player comes to the island, sweeps you off your feet, takes you to Europe."

"I'm so embarrassed." Holly covers her eyes.

"Why?" Miguel laughs. "These people love you. I bet it's like having a hundred grandparents or something. Which, honestly, would be kind of awesome."

"Yeah," Holly admits, "it is a little like that. Only they have opinions on everything I do, just like grandparents, and they meddle in my love life, just like grandparents."

"Hey, things could be worse," Miguel points out. "You live on a tropical island where everyone cares about your happiness. You're basically living the dream."

"You have a good point," Holly says. She starts walking again. "And now that you know everything about my love life—or what used to be my love life—I think you owe me some personal details. Oh," she points at a tree, "Palmetto Palm. Grab a few leaves."

"I was supposed to find things for us, remember?" Miguel plucks a few leaves from the tree. "You can't help me."

"Don't change the subject, Cruz. I want to hear everything."

"Everything? Wow," Miguel says. "That'll take about ninety seconds."

"Really? No juicy relationships? No big, unrequited loves?"

"Holly, I'm only twenty-three," Miguel reminds her. "I don't even know if I can say I've ever been completely in love before."

Holly considers this. "I'm thirty-one and I don't know that I can say that, either."

They walk in silence for a moment, lost in their own thoughts.

"Okay, one time I really, really liked this girl. Her name was Nora. We dated for a year, but...it never felt quite right."

"Sometimes it doesn't feel right," Holly agrees. "Which usually means it isn't, in my experience."

"Exactly. Like, she was always trying to get me to do things I didn't want to do. She wanted me to go to college and that wasn't on the radar for me."

"You never wanted to go?"

Miguel drains the rest of his coffee. "I don't know. Maybe? But not the way she wanted me to go. I really wanted to work and help my mom, and I like working with my hands. Being in an office doesn't sound right for me. But she wanted me to think about the future all the time. I was only eighteen, you know?"

"Different paths," Holly says. "I've been there. Jake and I always disagreed about being on the island permanently. But this is home for me."

"He doesn't want to stay?"

Holly shrugs. "He doesn't seem to want to go, but we had plenty of discussions that revolved around 'is this it'? And for me, it kind of is. I'm happy here."

"This island is you. Honestly, I can't picture you anywhere else."

"Me either. I felt like the biggest fish out of water ever the whole time I was in Europe with River. That was all wrong. Even the time I spent in Miami while I was in college was hard. I never felt like the other people my age. I didn't want to party, I didn't care about city life, and all I really did was live for the next break so that I could come back here and be at home."

"With your hundred grandparents," Miguel says, smiling.

"Yeah. With all of these amazing people." Holly turns down the driveway that leads to her house. "You've never been to my place. Want to come in?"

Miguel stops and looks at Holly's bungalow. It's nestled in amongst the trees, not too many steps from the front door of Buckhunter's house, which he now shares with Fiona.

"Yeah, sure." He follows her up the steps. Pucci is sitting just inside the front door when she opens it, waiting to be greeted by his mistress.

"Hey, boy." Holly bends down and scratches her dog behind both ears. "Have you been good? Wanna go outside?" In response, Pucci walks through the open door and down the steps, disappearing out into the yard. Holly stands up again and faces Miguel. "Let's have something to drink."

In the kitchen, Holly pulls open the stainless steel refrigerator door to reveal her nearly empty shelves. On the top one, she's got a container of milk, four cans of Diet Coke, a lemon, and a lime. In the door is a container of orange juice and a bottle of mustard.

"Not a big eater?" Miguel cracks. He's standing behind her, observing the absence of anything edible.

Holly takes two cans of Diet Coke out of the fridge and grabs the lime. "Actually, I'm a huge eater. I just don't like to shop or cook."

"How do you live?" Miguel laughs.

Holly pulls a knife from the butcher block and slices the lime into wedges. She fills two glasses with ice from the freezer and squeezes the limes over them, then cracks the cans of soda. "I eat with Buck-hunter and Fiona sometimes, but mostly I get takeout from Jack Frosty's or the Jingle Bell Bistro. I live on pastries and coffee from Mistletoe Morning Brew when I get to work." She shrugs. "You know, a girl does what she has to do to get by."

"So you don't cook?" Miguel takes the can and the glass from her and pours his own soda. "Not at all?"

"No. Not really." Holly is less than impressed with her own lack of culinary skills, and her ability to get by without turning on a stove is something she accepts about herself. "But you know what I am good at?"

"What's that?" Miguel picks up his glass and follows Holly through the house.

"I make a mean mosaic."

She leads them out onto the lanai through the door and points at her shell wall, which is about half done. Over the past few years, Holly has collected shells along the beach as she walks, piecing them together on the wall of her lanai late at night when she can't sleep. Many nights find her out under the spinning ceiling fan on her screened-in lanai, her clothes stained with mortar and who knows what else, music playing as she focuses on the perfect spot to place her next shell.

"I had no idea you were handy."

"Oh, come on," Holly says with a disbelieving tone. "Who do you think did the heavy lifting around here before you came along? I can unclog drains and nail boards to windows when there's a hurricane warning. I know how to paint walls, clear brush, and sail a small boat."

"You know," Miguel says, taking a sip of his soda. "I'm honestly not surprised. You're a real mix of things."

"Like piss and vinegar?" Holly laughs. "That's what my grandpa used to say."

"Is that a real saying?"

"Yeah, it is." Holly tucks a stray hair behind one ear and sets her drink on the table. "You'd be surprised at the colorful sayings you pick up when you live your whole life around people who were born before WWII."

Miguel shakes his head. "I was thinking more along the lines of you being a mix of strong and pretty. I don't know—is that right?"

Holly thinks for a second and then nods. "Hey, that works for me!"

"I mean you can do anything around here—you run this island—but you're still a beautiful woman..." Miguel trails off. He looks embarrassed, like he hasn't meant to say that much.

"Thank you. That's a huge compliment." Holly forces herself to accept it without doing what she's accustomed to doing in these scenarios: arguing against the compliment by playing down her attributes. Instead, she smiles at Miguel. "It's nice to be thought of so highly."

They stand on the lanai together for a moment and then Holly breaks the silence. "We should probably finish gathering the scavenger hunt stuff, or we're never going to win."

Miguel drains his Diet Coke in one long gulp and sets the glass on the table next to Holly's. "Want to know a secret?"

"Yeah. Tell me."

"I don't really care if we win." Miguel's smile widens. "I just thought it would be fun to hang with you. And I was right."

Holly laughs loudly. "You are too full of flattery, Mr. Cruz," she says. "But I like it. Don't stop."

"Okay," Miguel says with a poker face. "I won't."

"Good. Now let's dig up my signed copy of Jantzen Parks' new novel and pretend like we're in it to win it."

That evening's festivities include a full dinner at the Jingle Bell Bistro overlooking the water. The night air has grown windier and brought the slightest chill to the island, so half of the guests have chosen to eat inside, while the remainder are seated outside on the patio with candles flickering in hurricane lamps and sweaters wrapped tightly around shoulders.

"I heard that the elf was shtupping the author," says an older woman with a diamond the size of a marble on her ring finger. She holds a martini glass in hand and whispers loudly to her table companions. "Remember that murder mystery we did in Tallahassee? Same thing. The dead girl was engaging in extracurriculars with the main suspect. It's always the lover." She puts the glass to her heavily-glossed lips and knocks back the gin and vermouth like it's water.

"I don't know, Paula." Another woman with a permanent frown between her brows looks on disapprovingly while her friend scans the room for someone to bring another martini. "Sometimes it's a business associate. Or someone with a grudge."

"Hmph," Paula says. She twists the large diamond ring around on her finger and raises an eyebrow. "I've been with enough men to know. They'll put that thing anywhere they can, then do whatever they have to do to cover their tracks. I say it's the author."

"But what about Santa?" the friend asks.

"Easy," Paula says, spreading her hands wide. "He saw the author kill the elf, so he had to go, too."

The third woman at their table is the excessively nipped and tucked woman from Jack Frosty's, and Holly listens closely as she clears her throat. "I think you're both wrong," she offers, leaning back as Iris Cafferkey sets salads on the table in front of each of the three women. "And thank you," she says to Iris, casting a perfunctory glance in her direction. "I think the author is innocent," she says to her friends, leaning in closer. She picks up a fork. "I'm wondering if the doctor or the cop are in on it somehow."

Holly turns her attention back to Bonnie, Cap, and Heddie, who are sharing her outdoor table. She pulls a freshly baked roll from the basket on their table and reaches for the butter dish. This murder mystery weekend is turning out to be more fun than she'd anticipated, and while there is some work involved for her, amazingly she's been able to relax and enjoy it far more than any other event she's hosted on the island.

"You got any good ideas about whodunnit, Mayor?" Cap asks. He picks up a bottle of red wine and begins to pour it into the glasses of his table mates. Beyond the patio, the ocean roars on its approach, crashing loudly on the shore and retreating towards the lavender and blue horizon.

"I'm not sure," Holly admits, holding her glass while Cap fills it. The smell of steak and pot roast and fresh bread wafts from the kitchen out to the patio and Holly's stomach grumbles. "I have to be honest and say that I'm enjoying the whole idea of the murder mystery more than I'm concerning myself with how to solve it." She takes a big swig of wine and immediately feels the way it fills her empty stomach with warmth. To counteract its effects, Holly bites into her buttered bread.

"I have ideas about it," Heddie says in her thick, German accent. "I know a murderer when I see one, and believe me, there is a murderer amongst us."

"That's my cheerful little love bug," Cap says, reaching across and putting a hand on Heddie's arm.

"It's true," Heddie argues. "We are Germans, Cap." She looks at him as though he needs to be reminded of this fact. "Our noses are made to sniff out danger." Heddie puts one long, elegant fingertip to the end of her nose.

Cap chuckles at this and pours himself a glass of sparkling water instead of wine. "If you say so."

"Well, I don't know about you all," Bonnie pipes up, "but I think Mr. Jantzen Parks is completely innocent."

Holly drinks more wine and feels her tongue begin to loosen with each sip. "Jantzen Parks might not have killed anyone," she says, leaning towards Bonnie and wiggling her eyebrows, "but that man is guilty of committing crimes of *love!*"

Bonnie gives Holly a pitying look. "Honey," she says calmly. "Eat some more bread. Dinner is coming."

"Where is he really, Bonnie?" Heddie takes a sip from her wine-glass. "You must know where Mr. Parks is hiding."

"I've been sworn to secrecy," Bonnie says, holding up a hand. "But

I will tell you, this game is F-U-N *fun*! There's just something about having to keep a romance under wraps that really lights my fire."

Holly has taken Bonnie's advice and is chewing a hunk of bread to soak up some of the red wine. "Bon, your fire is always lit," she says, reaching for the butter dish to slather her next piece of bread.

"Sugar, you hush with that," Bonnie says, giving Holly's hand a playful swat. "We need to focus on the murder mystery here and forget about my love life for a minute."

"We could focus on Holly's instead," Cap offers, lifting his glass of sparkling water. "Any new prospects?"

"Miguel," Heddie says confidently. "He's a prospect."

"He's only twenty-three," Holly counters. "And a good friend."

"Pshhh." Bonnie swirls the wine around in her glass as Iris arrives at their table with four plates of delicious-looking food. "You know seven or eight measly little years won't be a dealbreaker when it comes down to it."

"But there is no deal to break!" Holly sits up straight as Iris puts a steak and a pile of mashed potatoes in front of her. "Miguel just moved here and I'm showing him the ropes. We work together basically everyday on different projects around the island, and he's turning out to be a great friend." She picks up a steak knife and a fork and starts to cut her meat. "Wait," Holly pauses, "why am I even explaining this?"

"I don't know, doll, but I'm all ears!" Bonnie giggles like a school girl hearing a particularly juicy piece of gossip. "Tell me everything."

Instead of responding, Holly jabs a piece of steak with her fork and shoves it into her mouth. She shoots Bonnie a look as she chews.

All around the patio and inside the restaurant, people are cutting into their meals and talking over drinks to the sounds of the waves on the beach. For a moment, it seems that there is no murder mystery to solve, and that all of the unfamiliar people dining at the Jingle Bell Bistro are just guests visiting the island for a quick getaway. The railings of the patio are wound with colorful Christmas lights, and inside of the bistro is a tall tree decorated from top to bottom with glass ornaments dipped in glitter.

It's almost Christmas, and the world feels peaceful and calm to Holly as the ocean soothes her and the food fills her formerly cranky stomach. She smiles at Cap and Heddie and even at Bonnie, who has tucked into her own baked chicken with vigor and is laughing at something that Cap has just said. Who cares if they all think she's going to date Miguel? Holly hasn't entirely decided how she feels about him beyond what she's already told everyone, and that's that they're just good friends.

She slices off another piece of the perfectly cooked steak and bites into it. Whatever happens with Miguel happens. Holly picks up her glass of wine and takes a big sip, watching the waves crash on the shore just feet from where she sits. Right now she's got everything she wants and everything else will have to wait.

8

AFTER DINNER, THE GUESTS WHO ARE STILL STANDING START AT Mistletoe Morning Brew, picking up coffees and hot chocolates to go as they take a moonlit tour of the island. Talk about Santa and Molly the elf fuels the buzz in the air, but Holly is more focused on how beautiful her island looks at night.

"And is it true that the decorations stay up all year?" A young Alpha Chi Omega bumps Holly with her elbow as she admires the overabundance of decor up and down Main Street.

"We do keep some holiday decorations up all year," Holly says, "but we change them out seasonally as well. For Halloween we do black and orange, and for the 4th of July we have red, white, and blue. But it's mostly Christmas stuff, yeah."

"Wow," the woman says, tipping her head back and looking up at the dark night sky. "I love this place." Her voice is full of awe. "You all are so lucky to live here."

Holly's gaze follows the woman's as she admires the Christmas lights twinkling against a backdrop of stars in the clear sky. "We are," she agrees. "We definitely are."

"Okay!" Margo says, clapping her hands to get everyone's attention. "We're taking a group walk around the island this evening and caroling as we go. Keep your eyes open for clues and feel free to discuss the investigation, and if you have any questions about the island and its history," she says, holding out a hand towards Holly, "Christmas Key's mayor and longest resident is here with us."

By now everyone knows who Holly is, but she raises her paper cup of hot chocolate anyway, acknowledging the introduction.

"Mind if I join you, Mayor?" Miguel steps up to Holly.

"Did you get a drink?" she asks him.

"I'm good." Miguel holds up a hand. "I just wanted to sing Christmas carols and see the lights."

"Then walk with me," she says as they begin to follow the crowd of about twenty people up Main Street. They make a right onto Ivy Lane and everyone oohs and ahhs over the strings of lights in the palm trees. Iris and Jimmy have—as always—gone all out, and their bungalow is draped in icicle lights. Their front yard boasts a gigantic snowman that lights up and plays "Frosty the Snowman," and several hot pink flamingos have been draped in Santa hats and red-and-white striped scarves. All of their trees are wrapped in multi-colored strands of lights, giving the yard the overall appearance of a carnival ride.

Mailboxes are adorned with wreaths all along the street, and nearly every front door is ringed with lights or wrapped in shiny paper and a giant bow like presents.

"Any more ideas on the murders?" Miguel asks, walking closely enough to Holly that their shoulders brush one another.

"I should have more ideas," Holly admits, "but I think I overdid it a bit on the wine at dinner and forgot to come up with any new theories."

"Man," Miguel says, shaking his head, "you are really living this up. Bonnie told me that you're normally too involved in planning and that you get stressed out by the events you put on. But this one seems to suit you."

"I'm having a good time." Holly shrugs. "And by now I think we've hosted enough events that I know which parts to stress about and which parts to just enjoy."

"So let's talk murder," Miguel says with a gleam in his eyes. "Jantzen Parks is still missing. And Santa and Molly Tucker are dead."

"Okay," Holly says, narrowing her eyes. Miguel is right: she is thoroughly enjoying the weekend, but her mind keeps wandering when it comes to solving the murders and she really wants to focus and participate in the game. She takes a sip of her cocoa. "You got my text to the group chat, right?"

"The one about Bonnie and Jantzen Parks?"

"I'm not trying to wreck the game, but if we're going to win, then we need to have the hard facts. Bonnie says Jantzen is here and innocent."

"But," Miguel counters, "isn't it possible that her judgment is clouded by love?"

"Or lust," Holly says.

"Oh! Look at that Santa on the roof!" The woman Holly has come to secretly think of as Plastic Surgery Lady is pointing at the enormous inflatable Saint Nick that Logan Pillory climbed up on top of his great-grandfather's house to set up. Santa's belly billows from the forced air that blows through his fabric body, and his jolly face grins down at them all, lit from within by a bright, white light. "I'm coming back here every Christmas," she says to the woman walking with her.

"So do we have any actual guesses so far?" Miguel prompts Holly.

Holly passes her hot chocolate from one hand to the other and thinks. "Well, I do think there's something to be said for a romantic angle. A crime of passion isn't out of the question in my book."

"You think maybe Santa and Molly were having a fling and he killed her?"

Holly weighs this idea, tipping her head from side to side as they stroll along with the group. They're currently bringing up the rear. "Maybe. But then who killed Santa? You think the stress of killing his lover sent him to the edge and he had a heart attack?"

Miguel laughs. "Wait, this is weird."

"What is?"

"Talking about Santa having some side action. And actually killing her."

Holly chokes on her drink and Miguel slaps her on the back. "*Santa having some side action?*" she splutters. "Did you seriously just say that? I can't..." Holly bends at the waist as Miguel continues to pat her back. They start to cackle together and a few of the women turn back to see what the commotion is about.

"Okay, first caroling stop!" Margo turns to face the group and holds up both hands. They're standing at the end of Ivy Lane. "I'm going to ring my bell and see if we can get anyone to come out of their homes." As she says this, she pulls a handbell from the pocket of her coat and begins to jingle it loudly. Doors open up and down the street and within minutes, Katelynn and Logan have led Hal Pillory out of the house, each holding him by an elbow. They stand on their porch and Jake steps out behind them, giving Holly a wave. She raises a hand in greeting.

Iris and Jimmy pull up to their bungalow in their golf cart with Emily in the backseat, all three looking tired from putting on the evening's dinner at the bistro. They turn off the cart in their driveway and stand in the yard, listening.

A few other doors open and people trickle out.

"Our first song," Margo says, "is 'Rudolph the Red Nosed Reindeer.'" The group pulls folded papers out of pockets and turn pages until they find the lyrics for the song. Holly coughs one more time, trying to swallow the fit of giggles that Miguel has started in her.

It takes a few lines of the song, but before she knows it, Holly is lost in the lyrics. Miguel is next to her, singing in a strong, clear voice that's more melodic than she expected. Holly wraps both hands around her warm cup of cocoa and puts her heart into it, singing with feeling. When the song ends, the group merges seamlessly into "White Christmas."

Everyone on the street applauds and cheers as the group wraps up their caroling with "We Wish You a Merry Christmas." Holly bumps Miguel with her hip. "You're a good singer," she says.

"Funny, you sound surprised. I am a man of many talents."

"I have no doubt," she says, realizing as she says it that it sounds more suggestive than she'd intended. "Should we keep walking with the group?"

"Yeah," Miguel says. "I haven't seen everyone's lights at night yet. This is pretty." They start walking again, rounding the bend onto December Drive and trudging through sand alongside the other carolers.

Holly puts her free hand into the pocket of her sweatshirt and holds her drink in the other. For a second, she'd kind of hoped that Miguel would want to break off from the group and wander the other direction on December Drive with her, but she's actually glad that he wants to stick with everyone else. Even though the wine from dinner has worn off, her judgment feels slightly blurred. She takes another drink of her lukewarm cocoa, remembering the things that Heddie and Bonnie had said at dinner about her and Miguel.

It's true: the eight years between them isn't enough to make Holly completely disregard him as a possibility, but the fact that he's living on the island gives her pause. After all, she and Jake have had to make major adjustments and reconfigure their relationship entirely following their break-up, and, truth be told, she isn't sure she wants to go through that again. She sneaks a glance at Miguel's handsome profile, at his slightly crooked but adorable nose, and at the way his earlobe turns just up slightly at the tip where the cartilage gives way to skin.

He's incredibly attractive—no question. But is she ready to go down that path again? *And furthermore*, she reminds herself, *does Miguel even want that?* Maybe not. Maybe he thinks of her as a friend, a buddy, a big sister. Her face flushes in the darkness and she's grateful that Miguel can't see her skin turning pink as she thinks of him that way. She takes a step to the left to put a tiny bit of distance between them.

The group is about to make another right onto Pine Cone Boulevard to wind back down to Main Street when they come up on a golf cart. From behind, two figures are outlined under the light of the moon, their bodies close together as they embrace in what can only be described as a romantic clinch.

A few of the women giggle and point; Holly is sure it must be Bonnie and Jantzen Parks and she almost pulls her phone from her pocket to text Bonnie quickly and warn her that Jantzen's cover is about to be blown. Instead, Margo gives a bark of surprise as she approaches the cart.

"Oh, my!" she cries, putting a hand over her heart. The people in the cart turn around in surprise, coming face-to-face with the group.

A ripple of noise fills the air as everyone realizes what's happening.

"Get out of here," Miguel says in disbelief. He puts a hand on Holly's arm. "No way. Isn't that..."

"Yeah, it is," Holly says. "It's Mrs. Claus. And that's Nigel Winters, Santa's business manager."

"Holy Christmas..." Miguel gives a low whistle.

Holly nearly drops her cocoa. "You got that right."

9

"So Mrs. Claus and Nigel Winters were…" Ellen trails off as she pours another coffee and hands it across the counter of Mistletoe Morning Brew the next morning.

"Yep. They were canoodling," Holly confirms. "Absolutely."

Ellen's wife Carrie-Anne gives a low whistle. "The merry widow was already enjoying herself, huh?"

"So it seems." Holly sets a five dollar bill on the counter and takes the whipped cream covered confection that Ellen passes to her in a plastic cup with a domed lid. "We're all meeting in front of the chapel this morning to share info."

Jake throws open the front door of the coffee shop and walks in wearing his uniform. He's holding his hat in one hand.

"Morning, Officer Zavaroni," Cap says in greeting. "Been an eventful weekend so far."

"Indeed it has." Jake holds onto the bill of his hat and hits his other hand with the cap as he stands in line.

"Hey, Jake." Holly nearly runs into him as she turns around with her drink in hand. "You joining us at the chapel?"

"I thought I might. I'm hoping to win Best Costume at the awards ceremony, so I need to be seen as much as possible," he says, holding out his hands so that Holly can admire the outfit he wears nearly everyday.

"I think you're a shoo-in. Unless Mrs. Agnelli beats you with the denim skirt she wore to Jack Frosty's when Buckhunter let her play hostess for five minutes."

Jake's smile widens. "Are you serious? She was wearing a jean skirt?"

"And a Hawaiian shirt," Holly says. "I loaned them to her and she actually looked really cute."

"I'm sure she did. I've just never seen her in anything but the kind of stuff my grandma would wear."

"Well, watch your back, Zavaroni. You've got competition for that award."

"Okay, I'll see you at the chapel in a few," Jake says. He shoves his cap into the back pocket of his cargo shorts and steps up to the counter to place his order.

"Holly. Just the woman I was looking for." Vance Guy is out of breath as he waves at Holly outside the coffee shop. He's got his key stuck in the door of A Sleigh Full of Books and a box at his feet.

"What's up, Vance?" Holly puts one hand against her forehead to shield her eyes as she looks at him. Her cold coffee drink is in the other hand and she stands next to him, watching as he twists the key in the lock.

Vance stands up straight and faces Holly. "I heard my mother caused quite a commotion at Jack Frosty's yesterday."

"Oh," Holly says, waving a hand. "That was Mrs. Agnelli's fault. I'm sure everyone has already forgotten about it."

Vance looks around like spies might be listening to their every word. "It's just," he says, lowering his voice. "My mom is a really private person. And Mrs. Agnelli had to have gotten way under her skin for her to admit that in front of everyone. She swore me to secrecy when she moved down here, even though I told her that no one would care at all about her and Denise. But she insisted that Calista and I keep it to our ourselves."

"Vance," Holly says, putting a hand on his arm. "I understand.

Maria Agnelli knows how to poke the hornet's nest, and she's been trying to get a rise out of your mom for quite a while now."

Vance sighs deeply and visibly relaxes. "Yeah, she has. We've been trying hard to fit in here, but it's not easy being the new people on an island where most people have known each other for decades."

Holly nods. "Understandable. But I hope you feel welcome here —everybody loves you guys."

"Oh, definitely," Vance says. "People have been great. But we've also brought the only two kids to the island—rambunctious ones, at that— and a cantankerous older woman. So there are times when I feel like we stick out, yeah."

Vance pulls the key from the lock and slides it into his pocket. He bends forward and picks up the box next to his feet.

"Just the other night Miguel was saying something really similar about being new and trying to fit in. So you're not alone there," Holly says.

"Maybe my man Miguel and I should have a beer some night and compare notes." Vance smiles at her and leads the way into the bookstore. "But in the meantime, I want to mitigate the damage between my mom and Mrs. Agnelli. My mom needs to feel like outing herself in front of the whole island wasn't a huge mistake."

"It wasn't—definitely not!" Holly sets her coffee on the little counter next to the register and hands Vance a pair of scissors from a cup as he wrestles with the packing tape on the box. "She should feel free to be who she really is here."

Vance slices through the tape and pops open the flaps of the box. Inside is a stack of books. "That's what I told her. But she hasn't left the house since her run in with Mrs. Agnelli, and I'm worried for my marriage if she refuses to set foot outside again."

Holly chuckles. "Yeah, Calista won't like that."

"You think you can help me convince her that everything is cool?" Vance takes the top book and sets it on the shelf.

"Sure." Holly picks up her coffee and pulls on the straw, jabbing it in and out of the drink as she mixes in the whipped cream. "I can try."

"That would be amazing. She's at home with the boys today," he says gratefully. "I mean, if you have a chance to swing by."

Holly looks at her watch and takes her first drink of the cold coffee. It hits her brain with the force of a wrecking ball and she taps her forehead with one fist as she squints against the brain freeze. "I'll head over now," she says. "Maybe I can talk her out of the house before I head over to the chapel and single-handedly solve this murder mystery."

Vance has his back to her as he shelves all of the books from the box. "Hey, good luck, Mayor—on both counts. I think you're gonna need it."

"IDORA?" HOLLY KNOCKS ON THE DOOR TO THE GUYS' BUNGALOW AND calls out for Vance's mother. "It's Holly!"

After a minute or two, the door cracks. "Mayor," Idora says, not opening it all the way. "Can I help you?"

"I wanted to talk to you. Can I come in for a second?" Holly's coffee drink is still in the cupholder of her golf cart, and she's already longing for the hit of caffeine she counts on in the morning to keep her gears grinding.

Idora takes a deep breath and steps back, opening the door the rest of the way. "Come in." She glances around outside and quickly closes the door behind Holly. "Vance and Calista are both working this morning and the boys are still sleeping." Idora tightens her robe around her body and pats her slightly mussed hair. "Can I get you a cup of coffee?"

"I'd love one," Holly says, already forgetting about her cold coffee. She follows Vance's mother into the neat little kitchen and sits in a wooden chair while Idora brews a pot.

"So what can I do for you?" Idora's back is still to Holly and her shoulders are straight and proud. On the refrigerator are family photos and hand-drawn pictures that Mexi and Mori have made.

"I wanted to talk to you about what happened yesterday." Holly fiddles with a cloth napkin that's folded and resting on a clean placemat in front of her.

"No." Idora holds up one hand but keeps her back to Holly. She's staring at the coffee pot as it drips and percolates. "I don't want to say anything more about that."

"Okay, then don't say anything." Holly forces herself to keep talking and not to let Idora's closed-off stance intimidate her. "I just wanted to come over and let you know that you have absolutely no reason to feel..."

"Ashamed?" Idora spins around and faces her, holding onto the counter behind her with both hands. "I don't feel ashamed, Holly. I feel like someone dragged me out into the sunlight when I didn't want to be there. I feel like I was forced to tell the world something that was mine to keep to myself."

"I understand that." Holly presses her lips together and looks down at the placemat. "I do."

"Do you?" Idora's words are confrontational, but her tone isn't; she simply sounds sad. "I came here and gave up the life I called my own to help my son and to be near my grandsons, but I didn't want to give up my privacy. I had the right to live the way I wanted to, and that old crow forced me to defend myself."

"Mrs. Agnelli never should have—" Holly begins.

"No, she had the right to pester me a little. That's fine. But she didn't have the right to get in my head, and I let her. Now my life is an open book, and here I am, having to figure out how to walk down the street with my head held high when everyone knows my business."

"I promise you," Holly says, holding up a hand like an oath. "Everyone knows everyone else's business on this island already. We all have to suspend our disbelief on a daily basis and walk down the street with our heads held high knowing that there are no secrets on Christmas Key."

Idora actually chuckles a little at this. "I suppose." Her eyes are faraway as she thinks for a moment. Behind her, the coffee pot beeps. "And I know you'll say that no one cares about who I love, yadda, yadda, yadda," Idora says.

"They won't!" Holly interjects quickly.

"Right—I get it. Ellen and Carrie-Anne have shown them that the idea of two women in love is nothing to be afraid of," Idora says, though she makes a slight grimace that says she hates the way people have to be carefully exposed to a lifestyle that doesn't seem out of the ordinary to her. "But I want you to understand that to people of a certain age—to my generation—it's still hard to be open about such things."

"I respect that." Holly nods at her and refuses to look away as Idora gives her a searching look. "I do."

Idora nods and turns back to the coffee, pulling two mugs from the cupboard. "Cream or sugar?" she asks, making it clear that the conversation about her love life has come to its conclusion.

"Cream, please." Holly takes the hot cup from her with gratitude and blows on the steaming coffee. "I need this. We've got a murder to solve today."

Idora tucks her robe around her ample thighs and sits in a chair across from Holly, holding her own mug of coffee in both hands. "The lover did it," she says.

"*Which* lover?" Holly wrinkles her nose as she takes her first drink of Idora's strong coffee.

"It doesn't matter, honey," Idora says, waving a hand. "Pick one. It's always the lover."

THE SMALL CROWD GATHERED AT THE CHAPEL THIRTY MINUTES LATER IS already abuzz with gossip and conjecture as Holly pulls her cart off onto a sandy patch of road near the church. The morning sun is parting the trees overhead, and while the temperature won't top seventy-two, several of the Alpha Chi Omegas are wearing nothing but tank tops and shorts with sandals. For the islanders, this "winter weather" means a slight chill in the air that calls for sweaters and jeans. Holly herself is dressed in a pair of olive green cargo pants, Converse, and a light blue sweatshirt with a hood.

"We've got questions and some theories," Jake says as Holly approaches. He tips his head towards a knot of women holding notebooks and pens. "That lady thinks that Margo and Hamlet are murderers who cover their tracks by running this whole show. She thinks Margo killed her first husband."

"What?" Holly laughs and shoves her hands into the pockets of her hoodie. "Who ever said anything about Margo's love life?"

"I think the woman next to her with the sun visor googled them or something."

"This is nuts." Holly watches the women as they lean close to one another, making points in hushed tones and comparing notes. "I had no idea that people would take this so *seriously*."

"All in good fun though, right?" Jake winks at her. "Hey, where's your partner in crime?"

"Which one?" Holly squints up at him as the sun crests the trees and hits her face.

"The redhead. I saw Fiona at the coffee shop and she's headed over here."

Holly glances around her. "No Bonnie yet?"

"That's why I'm asking."

"Let me call her," Holly says, pulling her phone out of the pocket of her cargo pants. She dials Bonnie's number.

"Sugar," Bonnie hisses. "I can't talk."

"Bon?" Holly walks away from Jake and turns her back to the crowd. "What's up? Where are you?"

"I'm with Jantzen Parks."

Holly smiles. This does not surprise her. "Okay, so why can't you talk?"

"Seems like we might be leaving the island for a bit. Things went to hell in a hand basket around here, doll."

"What?" Holly says this loudly and heads turn in her direction. She lowers her voice again. "What are you talking about?"

"Well, Jantzen's been hiding out here, as you know, just playing along with this game. But it turns out he might have killed that girl. Accidentally, of course," Bonnie adds.

"Wait—what girl? The elf?"

"Yes," Bonnie says emphatically. "*That* girl. But he swears he didn't mean to."

"Bonnie," Holly says, searching for the right words to bring her friend back to earth. "That girl isn't really dead. This is a *game*."

"Is it?"

"Yes!"

"How do you know she's not dead?"

"Bon, listen," Holly implores. "If she was dead, we'd know. Fiona never…"

Bonnie waits for a second. "Fiona never said whether she was really dead or not, did she?"

"Well, no, but…then where is she?"

"Your guess is as good as mine, sugar. But Jantzen is a respected novelist and I don't think he's got a guilty bone in his body. I need to help him."

"How are you two getting off the island?" Holly's forehead creases from a mild squint into a full frown.

"I'm not sure yet, but don't worry, honey. I'll be in touch."

"Bon," Holly says into the empty air between them. "Bon?" But there's no answer. Bonnie is already gone.

10

HOLLY IS TORN IN TWO TRYING TO DECIDE WHETHER SHE'S PANICKED OR entertained by this latest turn of events. The rational part of her believes that Bonnie and Jantzen Parks disappearing is yet another plot twist in the murder mystery, but there's another part of her that knows Bonnie well enough to imagine her friend sailing off into the sunset with a dashing man she's just met.

"Hi, Iris," Holly says as she takes the steps up to the B&B. Iris is on her cell phone on the sidewalk and gives Holly a wave with her fingers.

Inside the B&B, Maggie Sutter is manning the front desk. A romance novel is open and laying facedown on the counter next to a can of Diet Coke.

"Maggie," Holly says. She leans against the counter and pats it urgently with both hands. "When's the last time you saw Bonnie?"

Maggie takes her reading glasses off her face and sets them next to the book slowly. As she does, she turns her gaze to the ceiling as if searching for an answer. The process is slow and makes Holly want to reach across the counter and grab the older woman by both shoulders to give her a little shake.

"Let's see..." Maggie slides off the stool she's sitting on and straightens her shirt with both hands. "She was in here this morning, but she spent most of the time back in the office. Said something about looking a few things up on her computer."

Without another word, Holly pushes herself away from the desk and walks down the hall to her office. Inside, the morning sunlight streams in and fills the quiet space with warmth and dust motes. There's a to go cup of coffee on a coaster next to Bonnie's open laptop and the imprint of Pucci's furry body is visible on his dog bed in the corner. Holly's own desk chair is pushed in, her workspace neat. She walks around the desk and sits in Bonnie's chair. The screen has dimmed, but one touch of the power button brings it to life.

With a quick tap on the search bar, Holly brings up Bonnie's search history. She'd feel worse about this invasion of her friend's privacy, but these are their work computers, and at this point she just needs clues as to what Bonnie is up to.

"*Hair dye kits*," Holly mumbles to herself, smiling. She knows, of course, that Bonnie's red hair should be a bit more gray than it is, but seeing her friend's search for beauty products makes her smile. "*South Beach recipe diet tricks; photos of young Robert Redford; boats to rent; uninhabited Florida Keys*," Holly pauses. "Okay, now we're getting somewhere," she says aloud to herself. With a click of the mouse, she pulls up the page Bonnie had been looking at. It's filled with links to gorgeous, wild-looking islands, and each has the latitude and longitude listed beneath a photo.

Holly searches around Bonnie's slightly disheveled desk space for a notepad and pen. From beneath a printed page of figures and dollar amounts she pulls a small notepad. On it is written the words *Little Duck Key*. Holly knows that this is a quiet little island in the lower keys with boat docks and long stretches of sandy beach. Could Bonnie actually be sailing to Little Duck Key with Jantzen Parks? Is she so caught up in this murder mystery that she's willing to undertake a boat trip with a virtual stranger to an uninhabited key?

She rips the page off the notepad and folds it in half, sliding it into the pocket of her cargo pants. Her phone is in the same pocket, and she slips it out, dialing Bonnie one more time.

"This is Bonnie Lane. I'm not available right now, so please leave me a message—" Bonnie's honeyed Southern accent is playing in Holly's ear and she's debating whether or not to leave a message when a flurry of activity on the street outside her window catches her eye. She stands and sets the phone on the desk without hanging up.

"What the..." As she watches, Joe Sacamano, Buckhunter, Jake, and Carrie-Anne run by waving their hands and shouting. Holly's eyes move up the street to what they're chasing after. Madonkey, the donkey that Ellen and Carrie-Anne adopted to add to their menagerie of animals, has apparently gotten loose and is now standing in front of Poinsettia Plaza, pinning one of the Alpha Chi Omegas against the wide window of the beauty salon.

Holly puts all ten of her fingertips to her forehead and massages gently. She's not worried about the Alpha Chi Omega; Madonkey is totally harmless and happily nuzzling the woman's torso in search of affection and a snack. As she closes her eyes takes deep breaths, the group of islanders reaches the startled woman and successfully coaxes Madonkey away from her. There is laughter and relief on everyone's faces as Carrie-Anne leads the animal away with a series of handclaps and cooing noises. Jake attends to the woman, who is patting her hair and readjusting her purse across the front of her body protectively.

With a final rub to her temples, Holly collects herself and picks up her phone from the desk, ending the call and shoving it back into the pocket of her pants. More importantly than a donkey to corral or a murder mystery to solve, Holly now needs to get to the bottom of Bonnie's whereabouts so that she can stop her friend from making another ill-advised leap into romance. After Bonnie's brief move to the mainland to live with a kinky weekend pirate, she'd sworn to herself that she'd do everything in her power to keep that kind of romantic train wreck from ever happening again.

THE DINING ROOM IS STILL DECORATED FOR CHRISTMAS THAT afternoon, and several people are sitting at the round tables, sipping coffee or tea and talking in hushed tones. Mrs. Claus is perched on the edge of a chair near her late husband's ornate throne, staring at the red velvet seat as if he might suddenly materialize.

"Hi," Holly says to her, stopping near the table. "Mind if I sit?"

"Of course, honey. Sit. Please." Mrs. Claus pats her neatly combed white hair, smoothing the bun at the back of her head with one hand.

Holly sinks into the chair and puts her hands between her knees as she watches the woman pick at the table cloth absentmindedly. "How are you?"

Mrs. Claus lifts her gaze. "I'm getting by," she says.

Holly has decided that playing along with the whole act is the only way to really enjoy the game, but at the same time, she wants to dig for any information that might help her to locate Bonnie.

"I know this must be hard for you," Holly says, reaching out a hand and setting it on the older woman's wrist. She lowers her voice. "And it had to be embarrassing to get caught in the golf cart with Nigel Winters last night."

"That was a mistake," Mrs. Claus says. There's a sharpness to her tone that Holly hasn't heard before. "I was feeling lonely and scared, and Nigel has been our friend for a long time. He took advantage of that. There's nothing going on between us."

"I'm not insinuating anything, Mrs. Claus. I just wanted to express my sympathies."

Mrs. Claus gives a light sniffle and sits up straighter. "Well. Things are always more complicated than they look from the outside, dear," she says, the edge gone from her voice. "I'm sure you can agree, even at your young age, that affairs of the heart are never just a straight line, but more of a weaving, tangled web."

Holly thinks about this. Mrs. Claus isn't wrong: the overlapping and knotting of all her own entanglements would make a pretty interesting web. "True," she allows. "Were things going well between you and Santa?"

"We had the same issues that anyone who spends decades with

another person might have." Mrs. Claus puts one hand on top of her other hand and looks at Holly straight on. "Just because Santa is known for magic and toys and holiday cheer doesn't mean he isn't—" she pauses, "*wasn't* a man just like any other."

Holly nods. The image of Santa and Mrs. Claus spending the majority of the year living like any normal married couple is jarring. Disagreements over how to invest retirement funds. Hurt feelings when one isn't listening to the other. Mediocre sex. Bland casseroles. Parties with the in-laws that neither wants to attend. She tries to get rid of these thoughts.

"So—and forgive me for prying—things weren't great between the two of you?" Holly asks. She feels as though she's really asking someone for the intimate details of their relationship, when at the back of her mind is the realization that she's essentially playing detective by asking a well-trained actress questions about a fake marriage.

Mrs. Claus examines the puckered skin on the back of her hands before answering. "Santa was going through what's commonly known as a mid-life crisis," she says softly. "Only when you're Santa, you don't buy a sports car or join a gym."

"Because you already drive a sleigh and you can't afford to lose the belly," Holly says jokingly. Mrs. Claus gives her a serious look and Holly's wry smile melts away. "Sorry."

"It's not something I enjoy talking about," she says. Her eyes dart around the dining room, landing on Mrs. Agnelli and two of the triplets as they sip tea. "But Santa had recently..." she trails off and takes a deep breath, beginning again. "Santa had been seeing another woman. A younger woman."

Holly waits for Mrs. Claus to go on.

"It was one of his elves—the one you found in the author's room." Mrs. Claus hangs her head and Holly nearly forgets that this is all an act. "I'm so ashamed."

"Don't be. This isn't your fault."

With a deep inhale, Mrs. Claus lifts her head and looks into Holly's eyes. "It feels like it's my fault."

Holly reaches out and puts a hand on the woman's forearm. "Wait —I have one more question," she says, catching herself before she stands to go.

"Yes, dear?" Mrs. Claus' eyes flash beneath her white brows. In spite of her obvious age, her skin is smooth and plump, and her wrinkles are etched so finely that Holly isn't quite sure how old she actually is.

"What do you know about Jantzen Parks?"

Mrs. Claus sighs. "I don't read his books, honey. I wish I could tell you more, but I'm more of a romance novel kind of gal."

"Gotcha," Holly says, standing and pushing in her chair. "Thank you for talking to me. I really appreciate it."

"You're welcome, Holly." Mrs. Claus looks up at her as she straightens her cardigan and folds her arms. "You do such good work around here, honey. This is a lovely place to die." With a wan smile and a discernible spark in her eye, she turns her attention back to her late husband's empty chair again.

11

THE INSIDE OF NORTH STAR CIGARS IS RIPE WITH THE RICH SMELL OF tobacco leaves. From the back of the store, Holly can hear Cap Duncan whistling to himself and talking to Marco, the island parrot. Jimmy Buffet is playing over the speakers in the shop.

"Cap?" Holly calls out. The bell on the front door jingles loudly as she enters, but Cap keeps whistling and bumping around behind the wall that divides the front of the shop from the storeroom like he hears nothing. "Hey, it's Holly. Can I talk to you?"

"Mayor?" Cap pokes his head out of the back storeroom, and sure enough, Marco is perched on his shoulder, one alert eye turned to examine their visitor. "What can I do for you?"

"I need a little dose of reality."

"Then I'm afraid you've come to the right place." Cap walks into the front of the shop and gently transfers Marco from his shoulder onto a perch behind the front counter. "I've got about a much of a sense of humor as you'd expect from an old codger like me, but if you want a no-frills, to-the-point conversation, you're always right to find a German." Cap taps himself on the chest twice with his thumb. "We know how to be serious."

"Okay." Holly leans both elbows on the counter and eyes the

posters Cap has hung on the walls of his shop. "This whole murder mystery is making me feel like I only have one foot in reality."

"Good actors will do that," Cap says. "And these guys are pretty convincing."

"Yeah, I find myself buying into the idea that Santa keeled over in my B&B dining room, and that a young woman came to her untimely demise in one of my guest rooms. My mind is turning over the possibilities and trying to come up with an answer, but then something crazy like a donkey running down Main Street reminds me that I still have an island to run."

"Well, you're practical, so I can see where you don't buy into the hocus pocus entirely," Cap says, folding his arms across his strong torso. "But I know you've got a competitive streak, so the desire to solve this thing and win is probably strong."

"True. But then there's Bonnie. That's what I really need help with."

"Bonnie?" Cap's white eyebrows shoot up. "She seems like she can take care of herself, for the most part."

"Need I remind you of the pirate weekend?" Holly makes a face as she remembers Bonnie going overboard and throwing all caution to the wind on that brief romance.

"No, no," Cap says, holding up both hands. "You don't need to remind me. I spent months nursing Wyatt back from the edge after Bonnie nearly left us for good." Wyatt Bender's affection for Bonnie is well-known around the island and nearly everyone can see that he'd like to pursue something with her.

"I'm afraid it's happening again."

"She's fallen for a pirate?" Cap chuckles.

"No, a mystery author. Jantzen Parks swooped in and caught her eye, and now they've disappeared together."

"Disappeared? How so?" Cap pulls a cracker from a box and holds it up for Marco to take from his hand. "Are they holed up in her bungalow? Because I think we should probably keep that little tidbit from Wyatt if that's the case."

"It's worse." Holly pulls the folded piece of paper from the pocket of her pants and spreads it on the counter. "She called to tell me she was leaving, so I looked through her search history on her computer at work—"

"Wait, you can do that?" Cap's brow furrows with concern. "You can see what a person's been searching for?"

Holly gives a laugh at the look on his face. "Yeah, you can. Unless you clear your history."

"You wanna teach me how to do that, Mayor?" Cap makes a move to grab his laptop and Holly laughs again.

"I will, Cap. If you're really worried about Heddie finding out that you searched for ladies in bikinis, we can clear it out."

Cap leans in closer. "Shhh," he says, waving his hands back and forth. "The walls have ears!"

His very real look of panic makes Holly laugh even harder. "Okay, okay, give me your computer."

Cap logs in and passes it to her. "You are sworn to secrecy about the ladies in bikinis," he says, letting go of the computer reluctantly.

"Yeah, yeah. Don't worry about it, Cap." With a few clicks of the buttons, Holly clears his browser history and passes the computer back.

"Just like that?" He frowns at the empty search bar.

"Just like that." Holly points at Marco, who is preening and waiting for another cracker from his master. "Now, about Bonnie."

"Sure. Go ahead." Cap closes the computer and attends to the parrot.

"I found this note next to her computer with the words 'Little Duck Key' on it and her search history included some attempts to find an uninhabited Florida Key."

"Little Duck *is* uninhabited, but it's a popular visitor's spot. It's got boat docks and I think people even camp there sometimes. But are you sure they aren't just at her place with all the curtains closed? Did you check?"

"I know she's gone, Cap. She's impulsive and impetuous and crazy when it comes to love, so I believe her when she says she's left the island."

Cap sighs. "Okay," he says. He puts both hands on top of his head and smooths the flyaways that end in a hasty white ponytail. "Then we should probably head to Little Duck Key and see if we can find her. Don't you think?"

Holly ponders this. Leaving the island in the middle of an event and trying to bring Bonnie home isn't what she'd planned for this weekend. "Yeah," she finally says, shaking her head. "I think we probably should."

Cap stands up straighter and pats the counter with both hands. "Then let's get this show on the road, huh?"

Holly nods firmly. "Yep. Let's do it."

"Isn't it late to be setting out today?" Fiona asks, leaning over the table at Jack Frosty's as they consult the map of the islands together. She puts a finger on Little Duck Key, which is even farther towards Miami than Key West.

"We're taking the speedboat. It'll just be me and Cap."

"I don't know, Holly..." Fiona stands up straight and puts both hands on her hips. They've commandeered a corner table at the open bar, and Buckhunter is weaving through the tables, dropping off drinks and snacks. "What are you going to do when you get there? Spend the night on the boat?"

Holly stares at the map. "I'm going to grab Bonnie and shake her. Tell her to get her sweet behind into my boat and come back here with me rather than disappearing again with some strange guy."

Fiona nods without speaking. "Okay," she finally says, "but Bonnie is a grown woman and you're treating her like a teenager who climbed out of her bedroom window."

"You think I'm being dumb?" Holly chews on her lower lip and feels the inexplicable approach of tears. She fights to push them back.

"A little." Fiona is one of the best friends Holly's ever had, but she's also one of the most honest. "I think you and Bonnie act like mother and daughter sometimes, and you funnel all the love and concern you might normally have for Coco into Bonnie. You don't want her to leave you, and I totally get that. It's understandable."

Holly feels her skin flush with the realization that Fiona is right: she *does* have abandonment issues with Coco, and she *does* cling to Bonnie the way a girl might cling to her own mother. The tears that had been merely a threat before start to brim near her lash line.

"Hey, you're fine," Fiona says sternly. "This is just Psychology 101, and a totally normal thing. We want to hang onto those we love in any way we can, both for their own good, and for our own."

Holly begins to fold the map that Cap has lent her. "So you think I should wait her out?"

Fiona lifts her chin at Buckhunter to let him know that everything is fine; he keeps walking past their table. "I think you should let her have a break from the island if that's what she needs. Bonnie is a vivacious woman who loves to be in love. So let her be in love sometimes."

"Uggghhhh," Holly laughs. She swipes at the end of her nose with the top of her hand. The tears are minimal, and with her back to the restaurant she knows that no one besides Fiona can see her. "Okay, I'll tell Cap to stand down."

"Let's just finish this murder mystery thing and see what happens, huh?" Fiona puts an arm around Holly's shoulders and squeezes. "I feel like we've got some intense sleuthing going on by these Alpha Chi women, and someone is about to come up with an answer."

"You're right. Let's go."

12

THE SUNSET IS A BLAZE OF FIERY PINKS AND ORANGES OVER THE WATER as the group of islanders and guests sits around a bonfire. Holly has arranged for a casual hot dog roast that evening, and there are people walking along the water's edge with bottles of beer in hand, and others leaning over the fire as they roast hot dogs in the flames.

"So, crisis averted?" Miguel asks Holly as he approaches her with his hands in his pockets.

"Crisis?" Holly is bent over a cooler, rearranging the ice so that it covers the cans of soda and bottles of beer. She stands up straight.

"Bonnie. I heard Cap telling Jake that you guys were going to go and rescue her, but then you called it off."

"Oh, that." Holly is still slightly embarrassed about her overreaction to Bonnie leaving the island. "Yeah," she says, tucking her hair behind both ears. "I don't feel like we know much about Jantzen Parks, but hey, if Bonnie wants to go on a mini-vacation with the guy, then he's probably okay, right?"

Miguel shrugs. "Yeah, I'm sure he is." He watches Holly with an eagle eye. "Are you doing okay? It's a lot of work to put on an event like this."

Holly surveys the water. "It's actually been fun. This murder mystery is keeping me on my toes."

"I saw you talking to Mrs. Claus this afternoon at the B&B while I was puttying that hole in the wall by the door and repainting it. Did you get anything out of her? Any hints?"

Holly replays their conversation in her mind. "Well, she said that she and Santa had a relationship like any other—imperfect. And that she had no idea that Nigel Winters was going to put the moves on her in the golf cart. She said he took advantage of her in a weak moment."

"So Santa and Mrs. Claus bicker like anybody else's parents?" Miguel smiles and his dimple shows.

"I guess. But it seemed like there was something more..."

"Like she was hinting at real trouble?"

"Mmmm," Holly says. She wraps a piece of hair around one finger as she watches Mrs. Agnelli drop her hotdog into the fire and start swearing. "Maybe. I feel like I could figure this whole thing out if I just sat down and spent more time thinking about it. But I keep getting distracted by things like Bonnie leaving, Idora and Mrs. Agnelli throwing down at Jack Frosty's, and—"

"Me?" Miguel says, looking both hopeful and a little shy.

Holly blinks a few times. She's about to say that Miguel isn't distracting her at all, but she catches herself before the words come out. The unconscious filter in her mind catches before her mouth does that this reply will sound like a put-down. And in truth, she does spend a fair amount of time joking around and chatting with Miguel. He's been to her house, and they're always texting each other jokes or random things throughout the day. She blinks a few more times.

"Sorry," Miguel says, pulling a hand from his pocket and holding it up. "Don't answer that. I didn't mean to say that."

Holly snaps to and reaches out to wrap her fingers around his hand. "No, no," she says, shaking her head emphatically. "I didn't mean to just say nothing there."

"It's totally fine." Miguel smiles at her, but it's a more guarded smile than she's used to seeing from him. "I shouldn't have just thrown that out there."

Holly hasn't let go of his hand yet. "I love having you here," she says quietly, aware that people are wandering past them as they stand there. "You've been an unexpected and pleasantly surprising addition to the island and to my life."

"But?" Miguel looks away from Holly's steady gaze.

"But nothing." Holly is watching his face as he takes this in. "Christmas Key is small. I've made a few relationship mistakes, and I'm not desperate to make those same mistakes again. I'm busy and I'm happy, but it's always in the back of my mind that life can happen to you when you're least expecting it."

"I definitely didn't mean to bring up some awkward conversation in the middle of a bonfire," Miguel says, finally looking Holly in the eye again, though somewhat awkwardly. "I just really like you, Holly. You're a good friend to me, and I enjoy your company. A lot."

"Same," Holly says simply. "And I like to go with the flow." She squeezes his hand and then lets it go, but not before he nods in understanding. "You want a beer?" she offers, tipping her head at the open cooler.

"Love one." Miguel bends at the waist and pulls a bottle of Corona from the container, shaking off the ice and condensation. He uses the bottle opener that's built into the side of the cooler to flick off the lid. "You want me to walk around and see if I can get any other clues that might help us solve this mystery?"

Holly glances at her watch. "That would be good. I need to do a couple of things," she says, spotting Logan and his mom near the picnic table that holds all of the hotdog fixings. "See what you can find, yeah?"

Miguel puts the bottle of beer to his lips and gives Holly a sloppy salute with his other hand. As he walks away, she heaves a deep sigh of relief. The exchange blindsided her a bit, and she's hoping that she hasn't totally closed the door with Miguel. It's not that she's actively hoping that something will happen between them, but she honestly is fond of him, and in spite of their age gap and any other differences that might feel like obstacles, there is something about him that feels familiar. Something that brings her happiness every time she sees him or gets a text from him. Something that feels like...not necessarily destiny, but like possibility.

"Holly." Logan waves at her. He grabs Katelynn by the elbow and pulls her towards the cooler. "My mom wants to talk to you."

"I've been meaning to talk to you guys, too." Holly takes a few steps in their direction. "Hey, Katelynn. How's your grandpa?"

"He's good. Millie offered to sit with him for an hour or two so that we could come down here and mingle." The strain of caring for an aging grandfather with dementia is starting to show on Katelynn's face, though Holly deeply admires the dedicated way that Katelynn's adapting to full-time island life at the same time she's taken on the job of home-schooling her teenage son and managing her grandfather's care.

"I need to drop by and visit Hal soon," Holly says, as much to herself as to Katelynn. Hal Pillory has lived on the island almost as long as Holly has, and he and his late wife have played instrumental roles in her life.

"He'd like that," Katelynn says. "But right now this guy wants us to talk about some idea he's pitched to you." She reaches over and tugs on her son's right ear in a playful way. Logan dips his head to avoid her, his eyes never leaving Holly's face.

It's cute to Holly that Logan has such an obvious crush on her, but it's not entirely lost on her that he's only seven years younger than Miguel. The thought gives her pause, but she clears her throat and forges ahead.

"Yeah, he's got big plans to start a radio station here on the island," Holly says. She smiles at Logan.

"As you know, my grandpa's got a garage full of radio equipment." Katelynn slings an arm over her son's shoulders, though he's at least two or three inches taller than she is. "And Mr. Resourceful here has been lighting Google on fire with his searches for how-to manuals."

"I've also watched a ton of YouTube videos. I'm really good with the equipment. And Great-Grandpa says I can do whatever I want with it." Logan patiently tolerates his mom's public display of affection as he talks.

"Well," Katelynn says as an aside, "he'd probably agree to anything at this point—I'm not sure he even remembers that he has half of that stuff."

Holly nods respectfully. Watching Hal's mental state deteriorate has been difficult for everyone on the island. "True, but your grandpa has always been a very generous and giving person. I'm sure he'd be happy to have Logan learning how to use all of that equipment."

"You think so?" Katelynn lets her arm drop from her son's shoulders. "That's a relief to hear. You've spent more time with him than I have over the years," she says, her eyes full of regret. "And I don't want to move into his house and just take over like we own the place."

"I know he'd be tickled by Logan's plan," Holly assures her. "He taught me how to use most of that stuff when I was a bit younger than Logan—maybe eleven or twelve. We picked up stations from all over the South together and he taught me a lot about radio and technology. In fact," Holly says with a smile, remembering afternoons spent with Hal and Sadie Pillory, who'd been her teacher all through her years of schooling on the island, "your grandma let me earn science credit by working with him in his garage and figuring out how to make contact with other stations using that equipment."

"Are you serious?" Katelynn is clearly intrigued. "I love that you spent that much time with my grandparents."

Holly doesn't want to rub it in that she's had such close relationships with other people's families by growing up on the island under their watchful eyes, but the truth is, just like Miguel said, most of the older people have been surrogate grandparents to her for her whole life.

"Wow," Logan says, looking at his mom. "Holly probably knows as much as I do about Great-Grandpa's radio stuff."

"Well, I'm sure I've forgotten at least as much as you've just learned," Holly says. "But I'd love to get a look at it and see what comes back to me. I have a lot of really good memories of listening to college stations from Austin and Miami and discovering the music and bands that I still love."

"And what do you think about the radio station?" Katelynn asks. "Good idea? Crazy? Too involved?"

Holly ponders this. "Not crazy. Not too involved. And yeah, potentially a really good idea. Why not do the same thing your grandma did for me?" she says to Katelynn. "Give him some school credit for what he's working on. Let him find out what the FCC regulations are for starting a station and broadcasting live from the island. We've still got some empty space on Main Street, and we could set him up with a little spot to use as his station. There's an office above North Star Cigars with a little window that looks out onto Main Street."

"Wait, you'd let me have a place to set up?" Logan's face looks like he's about to short-circuit with excitement. "And I could broadcast and play music and everything?"

"Yeah," Holly says. "That's the whole idea, isn't it? And how amazing would it be for Christmas Key to have its own station?"

"Mom," Logan says, turning to face Katelynn. His voice is pleading. "Please, can I? I'll do all the work, I promise. And you can give me credit for something and it'll be like school work. And like a job, even though it doesn't really pay."

"Okay, okay," Katelynn says with a laugh. "Slow down a little, buddy. The wheels are turning for me, and if Holly thinks it's a good idea, then I'm definitely on board with us doing more research. Can you look into the legalities of it?" Her eyes search her son's eager face as he tries to keep his cool.

"Yeah, of course."

"Good," Holly interjects. "Then you do a bit more legwork while I see what kind of junk we'd have to move around in the little office over Cap's shop."

"You got it," Logan says, putting up a hand for Holly to high five him. She slaps his palm.

"I feel WXMS in our future," Holly says. She takes a few steps towards the bonfire. "Keep me posted, okay?"

Logan gives her two thumbs-up and Katelynn smiles at her son proudly.

Idora is sitting in a chair near the picnic table. She's got a can of

Diet Coke in one hand and she's leaning over towards another chair, chatting with two of the younger Alpha Chi Omegas. Holly raises a hand in greeting as Idora glances her way. Idora nods back and keeps talking to the young women. Holly is reasonably certain that the dust-up between Idora and Mrs. Agnelli will be forgotten before too long, but knowing both of the ladies as she does, the bad feelings might linger for a bit longer.

Holly keeps walking, and eventually she rounds the bend at Snowflake Banks, which is at the southwest corner of the island. If she keeps going, she'll wind up headed north, eventually ending up on the beach right beside her own property. Her intention isn't to leave the bonfire and the festivities entirely, but just to roam a bit and think. As usual, there's enough going on with general island life to keep her mind occupied during all of her waking hours, but having a B&B full of visitors and a mystery to solve has her brain on overdrive.

As Holly walks barefoot through the sand, a roseate spoonbill swoops in low and lands just a few yards ahead of her. She stops in her tracks and watches as the beautiful bird picks at a mollusk shell with its duck-like beak. The gorgeous hot pink of the bird's feathers makes it look like a flamingo, but its ability to take flight and soar against a cloudless blue sky means that it's most definitely *not* a flamingo.

The bird gets its fill of the shell and lifts off again, winging out over the water and putting space between itself and Holly. She starts to walk again.

In the distance—from around the bend—Hamlet and Margo are walking as fast as their age and physical restraints will allow, leaning on one another for support. Their faces look distressed.

"Mayor!" Hamlet calls out, waving a hand as if Holly can't see them. "We need you!"

"Get help!" Margo calls, flagging Holly down with both of her hands in an exaggerated SOS.

"What is it?" Holly breaks into a jog, trying to reach the older couple as quickly as she can.

Hamlet cups his mouth with two liver-spotted hands. "There's a boat that's capsized," he shouts. "And we have someone washed up on shore. Get help!"

Holly stops running. "Who is it?" she yells back. The blood drains from her face.

"The author," Margo calls out. "Jantzen Parks. He's not breathing. Get someone! Bring help!"

13

There are no words as Holly stands to the side, hands over her mouth, watching Fiona attend to Jantzen Parks. Holly had run as fast as she could after Hamlet and Margo had given her the news, and when she'd come back, she'd brought Jake, Fiona, Buckhunter, and Cap with her.

Cap and Jake are now waist-deep in the water and using a rope to pull the waterlogged boat to shore. Buckhunter has driven a golf cart to the spot on the beach where Jantzen is lying, and Fiona has turned him on his side and cleared his airway of water.

"But where is Bonnie?" Holly asks for the umpteenth time. "Is she out there?" She wants to drop to her knees and shake Jantzen Parks's limp body, but he's drenched from head to toe in cold water, his lips still an alarming shade of blue. Buckhunter jogs over from the golf cart with two blankets in his arms.

"Jantzen," Fiona says, wrapping him in one of the blankets that Buckhunter hands her. "I need you to give me an answer on this. It's vitally important." Fiona puts her hands on the author's face and turns it so that he's looking at her with his slightly vacant gaze. "Where is Bonnie? Was she with you on the boat?"

Jantzen makes a noise like a mewling kitten. For a man of his tall, imposing stature, he currently looks like a helpless jellyfish flopped on the sand.

"Was she out there with you when you capsized?" Fiona asks again, giving his shoulders a gentle shake. "If she was, we need to get out there now and search for her. You have to tell me."

In response, Jantzen starts to shiver violently. He squeezes his eyes shut and Holly nearly faints as she waits for an answer. She wants to berate him for attempting to man a boat when he clearly has no idea what he's doing, and to rail against the idiocy of trying to make it to another island in a boat that's clearly not equipped for the job. Bonnie should have known better, and the thought that she got roped into something so dumb because she was starry-eyed over a man who clearly shouldn't be in charge of anything more challenging than a keyboard and mouse has Holly in knots.

"WAS. BONNIE. WITH. YOU." Holly finally shouts, making it sound like a demanding statement instead of a hedging question.

Jantzen nods, his eyes still closed. "We left the island together," he says. These are his first words since taking a breath after Fiona's forceful chest compressions. His voice is raspy and filled with regret. "That's all I remember."

Buckhunter shouts at Cap and Jake as they're dragging the boat onto the sand. "We need to radio the Coast Guard. And start looking for Bonnie. She's out there."

Cap and Jake drop the rope they're holding and spring into action. Without asking, they jump behind the wheel of Buckhunter's golf cart and take off. Holly knows that as their maritime connection on the island, Cap will both send out a call for assistance and start searching for Bonnie himself. And without a doubt, Jake will be at his side.

"What were you thinking?" Holly asks, finally walking over to Jantzen and looking down at him. He pulls his knees towards his chest as he lays on his side, wincing in pain.

"He swallowed a lot of salt water," Fiona says to Holly. In her eyes is a tired doctor's warning to go easy on him, though she very clearly doesn't want Holly to let this man off the hook for putting Bonnie in harm's way.

"Where were you two going? Is this part of the murder mystery? What the hell is going on?" With each question, Holly can feel her blood pressure rising. She spins around to face Margo and Hamlet, wanting answers. The elderly couple are huddled together several feet away from the scene that's playing out.

Margo shakes her head; her eyes are wide and scared.

"Is this some sort of red herring?" Holly demands of them. They both stare at her mutely. "Are you faking this?" she asks Jantzen, turning back to look at him. "I need to know if you are. I'm the mayor of this island, and I don't mind a dead elf in my guest room or watching Santa keel over in my dining room, but when one of my very best friends might be out there in the water right now—" Her voice catches in her throat and a sob escapes. As her hands cover her face, Miguel and Logan come running up the beach.

"What the hell is going on here?" Miguel asks, stopping short of Jantzen's prone figure. He looks at Fiona's. "What happened?" Without hesitation, he walks over to Holly and grabs her by the shoulders. "Hey," he says gently. "What's going on, Hol?"

Holly shakes her head, keeping her hands over her face.

"Mr. Parks was on a boat that capsized," Buckhunter explains. "He washed up here, but Bonnie is missing."

Miguel's hands fall from Holly's shoulders. "Are we searching?" he asks. "Tell me where to go—is Cap heading out?"

Holly nods. Her hands drop from her eyes and she looks at Logan and Miguel. "He and Jake just left here in Buckhunter's golf cart. I'm sure they're going to the cigar shop and then leaving on Cap's boat."

"Got it," Miguel says. He reaches out and gives Logan a light punch on the shoulder. "Let's go help." The guys are about to turn and break into a run when Miguel pauses and reaches for Holly. He pulls her into a quick, reassuring embrace. "We've got this, okay?" he says to her, stepping back to look her in the eye. When Holly nods at him, he and Logan finally break into a run, disappearing back down the beach.

With Jantzen recovering under a blanket, Fiona walks over to Holly and pulls her into a much tighter hug than Miguel's quick embrace. "The guys are on it," she promises her best friend. "You want me to walk you home and we can wait for news there?"

Holly swipes at the tears that have started to fall. "No," she says. "I want to be where the action is. Let's go and see if Ellen and Carrie-Anne will open up the coffee shop and let us use it as home base. Maybe they'll even brew us a pot or two."

"I bet they will," Fiona says, turning her body so that she and Holly are side by side, but her arm is still around her friend's shoulders. "They're both at the bonfire. Let's go and make that happen."

COMPLETE DARKNESS FALLS OVER THE ISLAND. HOLLY IS STANDING anxiously next to a table in the center of the coffee shop, calling out questions and commands. Buckhunter has stopped at their shared property and picked up Pucci, who now sits at his mistress's feet, eyeing each person's approach warily.

Ellen and Carrie-Anne had agreed to re-open Mistletoe Morning Brew, and the place is buzzing with locals and visitors who have showed up to pitch in. The shop is decorated for December with a dizzying display of holiday lights and they're all plugged in now, twinkling and filling the room with color and warmth.

The coffee shop's theme for the month is *National Lampoon's Christmas Vacation*, and in keeping with the theme, there is a cardboard cutout near the front counter of Clark Griswold wearing a Santa costume, holding a chainsaw in one hand. In one corner of the shop is a fake tree that's too tall for the room, and its top is bent over and crammed into the ceiling just like the one in the movie. A stuffed chipmunk peers from the tree's branches, and a string of lights trails away from the tree, ending with a singed stuffed cat that's been made to look like the unfortunate feline who chewed itself right through an electrical cord and ended all nine of its lives in the film. It's a funny and charming send-up of a holiday favorite, and—as always—

everyone is impressed by the details that Ellen and Carrie-Anne put into their monthly decorations.

Right now, Iris and Jimmy Cafferkey are seated at a table under a poster from the film, manning their cell phones and parsing out information as it comes in. Holly has ensured that Jantzen Parks is safely ensconced in his room at the B&B and under Fiona's supervision, and as she rubs her tired eyes with one hand and holds a mug of black coffee in the other, one of the triplets leaves the table she's sharing with her identical sisters and comes over to give Holly a hug.

"Honey, that Bonnie is a tough old broad. We all know that. So I don't want you to worry about a thing until there's a reason to worry, okay?"

Holly nods as Gwen gives her a motherly squeeze. "Thanks, Gwen."

"Do you want to come and stay at my place tonight? You can bring Pucci if you like. We'd love to have you."

"Oh, you are too kind," Holly says. Her eyes fill with tears again. "But I'm okay right now. A little shaky, but I'll stay here until we know something, and then I'll probably just head home with Fiona and Buckhunter for the night."

"Well, the offer stands, sweetheart. Just say the word." Gwen puts a hand against the side of Holly's face and looks at her for a long minute before heading back to the table she's sharing with her sisters.

"Pour you another cup?" Ellen is standing next to Holly with a pot of coffee in one hand. Her eyes are tired and sympathetic. "You're burning the candle at both ends here, girl."

Holly sets her mug on the table so that Ellen can refill it. "I know. But I'm not going anywhere until we find Bonnie."

"I would expect nothing less." Ellen gives Holly's arm a squeeze. "We all know how much she means to you."

"Thanks, Ellen." Holly picks up her coffee and holds it in both hands. She eyes the clock on the wall: eight-fifteen. It's been a little more than two hours since Jantzen Parks washed up on the shore. "Iris?" Holly calls out. "Any word?"

Iris has her ear to the phone. She holds up one finger as she listens intently. The din in the coffee shop lessens as everyone gathers that Iris is listening to news of some sort. "Uh huh," she says. "Okay. Right." With a finger to the screen, Iris ends the call. She looks at Holly. "Head out to the new dock," she says.

Without waiting for another word, Holly sets her mug down and rushes out of the coffee shop. Pucci is at her heels.

Her pink golf cart is parked at the curb and she jumps into it, patting the seat next to her for her dog to join her. He jumps up and sits down just as Holly releases the brake and pulls out onto Main Street, doing a quick U-turn in the middle of the street so that she's pointed the right direction.

Between the massive amount of holiday lights on Main Street and her bright headlamp, Holly can see everything around her. People are streaming out of the coffee shop, heading to their own carts and making their way to the new dock on foot. Holly slows and comes to a stop. "Want to join me?" she asks Millie Bradford and Mrs. Agnelli as they start to walk with the rest of the group. The two women climb into the back seat and get settled.

When she reaches the new dock, Holly stops the cart and sets the brake quickly, jumping out and leaving Pucci to follow. A boat with a light on the front is zipping towards shore, and as it approaches, the U.S. Coast Guard insignia is visible on the side. It slows and approaches the new dock, and the captain eases the vessel in expertly. Holly is already standing on the dock when they arrive.

"Do you have her?" she calls out, her voice thick with emotion and impatience.

A woman in dark blue cargo pants and a dark blue shirt jumps off the boat. She's wearing a fitted orange vest over her shirt, and her hair is pulled back into a tight bun.

"Are you the island doctor?" the Coast Guard officer approaches Holly.

"I'm the mayor. Do you have Bonnie?"

The woman's eyes are light green and her face is youthful and serious. She looks at Holly's face intently. "We do."

Holly is ready to board the ship without invitation to see

Bonnie, but the woman holds out a hand. "She was in the water for quite a while. She's okay, but we need to make sure she's going to get the medical attention here that she needs. Is there a doctor available?"

As the woman is asking the question, Fiona is parking her own cart and making her way to the dock. "Do they have Bonnie?" she calls out anxiously. "Hi," she says to the Coast Guard officer. "I'm Dr. Potts. Did you find her?"

"We did, ma'am," the officer says. "She'd been in the water for approximately two hours, but was alert and coherent. Cold, but with it enough to give us her name and tell us exactly what happened."

"Can I see her?" Holly asks, unwilling to wait any longer for the details.

"Let's transfer her from the boat," the officer says, turning to motion to her crew.

Within minutes, they have Bonnie off the boat and on a flat stretcher, covered with a blanket.

"We can transport her to my office in a golf cart," Fiona says, motioning to where she's parked.

"Hi, sugar," Bonnie says to Holly. She reaches out a hand from where she's laying and the blankets fall away.

Holly crouches down next to her and takes Bonnie's hand. "Hey, stranger. I don't know whether to hug you or throttle you."

"I'd take a hug first," Bonnie says, tightening her grip on Holly's hand.

"I think we can get her upright in the golf cart for the trip," the officer says. She nods at the cart, and three of her crew join her in lifting the flat stretcher and carrying it up the sand. They set Bonnie down again and help her get from the ground to the seat of the cart, wrapping her tightly in a blanket again for warmth.

"I'm so relieved right now," Holly says, putting both hands to her temples and rubbing them. "I don't even know what to do or to think next."

"How about we just handle first things first," Fiona suggests. "Let's get her to my office for a full exam, and then we can decide whether you take her to your house for the night, or whether one or both of us need to stay with her at her place."

"Good idea."

"You want to follow me?" Fiona suggests.

"I'm right behind you, Doc." Holly gives her best friend a grim smile and gets ready for the long night ahead.

14

Holly is dozing on the couch in Bonnie's living room later that night with a thick quilt pulled over her tired body. She's given Fiona the guest room, and they're taking turns checking on Bonnie to make sure she's not feverish or in need of anything. The clock on the kitchen wall ticks loudly, filling the front of the house with an eerie reminder of the slow passage of time. A light from over the stove shines dimly into the living room.

Holly's cell phone vibrates on the coffee table next to her and she rolls over. She doesn't recognize the number.

"Hi, this is Wendy Villa from the *Miami Herald*," a woman says when Holly answers. "Is this Holly Baxter?"

Holly pushes off the quilt and sits up reluctantly. Her head is heavy with exhaustion. "It is."

"Hi, Holly. I'm calling about the capsized boat near Christmas Key today. I got your number from our advertising department, because you'd worked with us before to promote your island. Oh, and I'm sorry to be calling at such a horrible time," she adds, almost as an afterthought.

"It's okay. What can I do for you?" Holly rubs her eyes.

"I wanted to know if I could get a bit more detail on the search and rescue. I heard Jantzen Parks was involved, and the whole thing sounds like it'll make a great human interest story in the Sunday edition of the *Herald*. But if I'm going to get it out before tomorrow, I need to jump on it. Would you mind answering a few questions?"

Holly agrees and fills Wendy in on the murder mystery weekend and how Jantzen and Bonnie had capsized and been rescued. She leaves out the fact that Bonnie was acting like a lovesick teenage girl trying to escape from her room with a boy, instead making it sound like a local had agreed to give one of their esteemed guests a quick boat tour of the island. No reason to make it sound like anything other than a fluke accident during a totally normal outing.

"Thank you so much, Holly. I've got a quote from the Coast Guard already and a picture of Christmas Key on file, so I think this should do it. The story will run tomorrow."

"No problem," Holly says. She ends the call and sets her phone on the table again, then lays back down and pulls the quilt over her. This time, within minutes, sleep overtakes her.

THE SMELL OF COFFEE WAKES HOLLY FIRST. THE SECOND THING SHE notices is the bright morning sun streaming in through the blinds in Bonnie's living room. Somehow she's managed to get about five hours of sleep.

"You girls want some coffee? Can I make you a big southern breakfast?" Bonnie is up and bustling around her kitchen.

"Bon!" Holly throws the quilt off of her and swings her legs around so that her feet touch the floor. Her neck cracks as she tilts her head from side to side. Her back feels like she slept on a piece of wood. "What are you doing?"

"Getting my morning started, sugar. What are you doing?"

Holly stands and reaches overhead, stretching her spine. "I was just holding my post out here in the front room to make sure you didn't try to sneak out at night and get into mischief," she teases.

"Funny girl," Bonnie says with a smirk. "Now can you come in here and open this carton of milk for me? The lid is stuck tighter than a hair in a biscuit." Bonnie is bent over and trying to unscrew the top on a gallon of milk.

Holly takes the jug from her and easily removes the lid.

"Huh." Bonnie eyes the offending beverage. "Must be my hands are still a little tired from all that treading water."

Just the mention of Bonnie out in the cold water for hours makes Holly's blood start to rush. She takes the few steps over to the kitchen table and sits down. "I still can't believe this happened." Holly pulls her messy hair into an untamed bun at the back of her neck, securing it with the black hair tie she'd put around her wrist before falling asleep on the couch.

"All's well that ends well," Bonnie says in a cheerful voice. She tips the gallon of milk over her mug of coffee and pours. "Get you a cup?"

Holly nods and yawns. "Where's Fiona? What time is it?"

"Fiona was up early to check on me, and then she went over to the B&B to do another check on Jantzen. And it's nearly ten o'clock." Bonnie walks a steaming mug of coffee over to the table and sets it in front of Holly. As she does, her slippers make a pit-pat sound against the tile floor.

"I can't believe I slept till ten," Holly says. She lifts the mug and takes a sip. "Oh! And a reporter from the *Miami Herald* called last night and asked a few questions. They're running an article today about this whole thing."

Bonnie opens the refrigerator and scans its contents. "I hope they make it sound romantic," she says, pulling a carton of eggs from the shelf. She closes the door and pit-pats back to the stove.

For some reason, this infuriates Holly. "Bon, this was not *romantic*. This was *stupid*. You could have died last night."

Bonnie sets the eggs down and turns around. "Honey, everything turned out fine. I like Jantzen. He's smart and funny, and—"

"And you don't even know him!" Holly stands and pushes back the kitchen chair. "He's a total stranger, and you just take up with him like you're desperate for a man."

Bonnie blinks a few times like Holly's just slapped her. "Desperate? Is that what you think of me?"

Holly swallows hard. Her own words ring in her head. "Of course not. I don't think you're desperate, I just think you were *acting* like it. I felt like it was the pirate weekend all over again. Like I might lose you."

"Oh, sugar." Bonnie opens her arms and Holly walks over to her, falling into the embrace. "You will never lose me. So don't even try." She holds Holly close. "But I'm a woman who loves love, and I'm not going to stop being this way anytime soon."

"I know," Holly says. "I just wish you could love love with someone right here on Christmas Key and not fall for every dashing grandpa who shows up on this island."

Bonnie laughs and her upper body shakes. She's still holding onto Holly. "Every dashing grandpa, huh?" Her laugh continues as she runs her hand over Holly's head, which is resting on her shoulder. "Oh, you sweet ray of sunshine," she says, planting a kiss on top of Holly's light brown hair. "What would I ever do without you?"

"What would I ever do without *you*?" Holly squeezes her eyes shut tightly. "I don't want to find out, okay? So can you just give in and go out with Wyatt already?"

This makes Bonnie laugh again. "Oh, girl. If only life were that easy. You manage to fall for all the boys who show up on our island, and I manage to go head over heels for the ones who want to drag me away."

"I've only fallen for Jake...and River," Holly says. She pulls back from Bonnie and looks her in the eye.

"And what about this cute little dish you've been running around with lately?" Bonnie puts her hands on both sides of Holly's face and looks back at her just as intently. "You can't tell me there's nothing there."

"Are you talking about Miguel?"

"Sugar, don't act like you're blind in one eye and can't see out the other!" Bonnie cranks up her thick-as-molasses southern accent to go with the colorful saying.

"But, we're just friends."

"Mmmhmmm. I see that."

"Bon, he's way too young," Holly pulls away from Bonnie and sits back down. She picks up her mug of coffee again and shakes her head definitively. "Eight years is too much, isn't it?"

"Honey, remember Aunt Mildred and Uncle Jack? Thirty-two years between those lovebirds and not a damn one of those years made a difference."

Holly drinks her coffee and says nothing.

"Remember when I told you about them? In the B&B office a while back?" Bonnie brings her coffee over to the table and sits down across from Holly.

"Yeah. You said he wrote a book after she died."

"Well, I found it." Bonnie smiles at Holly over the rim of her mug. "You wanna read it?"

"Wait, you got your hands on the book that Uncle Jack wrote? How?"

Bonnie shrugs. "I asked Vance to track it down. I have no idea how he does his book thing, but he located a copy somewhere up in Virginia in a used bookshop and got it for me."

"Get out of town." Holly sets the mug down heavily. "Yeah, I want to read it! Of course. And not just because of their age difference," Holly says, making it clear that she isn't using it as a how-to manual for a May-December romance, as Bonnie had suggested when she first told Holly about it. "It sounds fascinating."

"It is." Bonnie gets up from the table and disappears down the hall. "I read it all in one night." Her voice trails out to the kitchen from the bedroom. "Stayed up till four a.m. and couldn't put the thing down."

"So he's a good writer?" Holly looks up at Bonnie as she enters the kitchen again, book in hand.

"A damn good writer." Bonnie hands over the tattered hardcover and sits back down. "And clearly smitten with Aunt Mildred, even after she'd passed."

Holly turns the book over in her hands and looks at the back cover. A good-looking man in his fifties stares back at her. He's got sandy blonde hair, a rakish smile, and the look of an intellectual behind a pair of smart tortoise-shell glasses. "Not bad to look at, either," Holly says as an aside.

"Read it, honey. It's worth a lost night of sleep or two."

"Thanks, Bon." Holly drains her coffee and stands up, tucking the book under one arm. "I should really get home and shower and get this day going. By the time the sun sets tonight, the murder mystery will be solved, Island Paradise Excursions will be here and docked so that our guests can depart, and we'll be back to business as usual."

Bonnie looks up at her with one eyebrow arched, her own cup of coffee held between both hands. "Holly Jean, you and I both know that there's no such thing as 'business as usual' around here."

"You're right, Bon. You are so right."

15

THE ALPHA CHI OMEGAS ARE GATHERED IN A BIG CROWD OUTSIDE OF Mistletoe Morning Brew by the time Holly gets there at noon. She's left Bonnie's house and gone home to shower and let Pucci out, and now that she's on Main Street dressed in jeans and a long-sleeved t-shirt and with her hair pulled back into a wet ponytail, she's ready to get down to business and solve this mystery.

"Hi there, Mayor," says Hamlet. He approaches Holly with both hands in the pockets of his seersucker slacks, jingling the coins and keys in his pockets as he walks.

"Hey, Hamlet." He's about four or five inches shorter than Holly and has a shiny bald patch on the top of his head that looks like a crater on the moon. "I like your bowtie." She nods at the green tie around his neck that's printed with tiny candy canes and bits of mistletoe.

"Thank you kindly, young lady." Hamlet takes his hands out of his pockets and straightens the tie smartly. "I always dress to impress."

"Always dressing to impress the ladies," says Margo, coming up behind her husband and putting a hand on his back lovingly. She's even shorter than he is. "Are you ready to pitch your theories and solve the mystery?" Margo asks Holly. "I bet you have some good ideas."

Holly squints into the sun. "I'm not sure that I do, to be perfectly honest. I thought I might, but I've gotten distracted by other things so many times."

"You do seem to have a lot going on here," Hamlet says. "How's the lady who had her love life dragged through the dirt in front of everyone?"

"Idora? Oh, she's fine," Holly assures them with a smile. "Occasionally we have a bit of a brouhaha here on the island over this or that, but when it comes down to it, there's a lot of love. We all have to live together, and we figure it out."

Hamlet goes back to jingling the contents of his pockets. "I can see that just from being here a couple of days. Special place you got here, Mayor. Good people."

Holly smiles at the couple. "Indeed. I never let a day get away from me without stopping to be grateful for all of this." Holly sweeps her hands around at everything.

"And what about Bonnie?" Margo asks, putting her palms together as if she's praying. "Is everything alright?"

"Bonnie is good." Holly gives a firm nod. "She's just fine. Fiona and I spent the night over at her place and this morning she was up and around, acting like her old self. To be perfectly honest, the long term effects will be on me, most likely."

"Gave you a scare, did she?" Hamlet places a grandfatherly hand on Holly's shoulder. "She's a real broad, that one. Gotta keep an eye on girls like that."

"Oh, Hamlet," Margo says, swatting at her husband. "You hush."

"No, I mean it," he says to his wife. "She reminds me of a dame I knew back in the day. Kind of a mix between Jane Russell and Marilyn Monroe. Only with red hair."

"Hamlet, you old trouser snake," Margo says. She gives him a pinch from behind in a place that Holly can't see, but given the way he jumps and the sly grin on his face, Holly has a pretty good guess. "Always looking at the ladies. What am I going to do with you?"

"Put up with me for the next fifty-three years, just like you've done for the last fifty-three."

"We'll see about that." Margo leans in close and gives her husband a chaste peck on the lips.

"I guess we have one more event to run before everyone breaks for lunch and then meets back in the dining room for cocktails, right?" Holly checks her silver watch. "The boat will be docked and ready to board around seven, and they should have you all back to Key West around eight-thirty or nine."

Margo puts her arm through her husband's. "Sounds about right to me. Should we get things started?"

"Can I have your attention, please?" Holly says loudly as she cups her mouth. The chatter on Main Street slows and then dies down. "If you're taking part in the 'Shoppin' Around the Christmas Key' event, we're going to start here at the east end of the island."

The Alpha Chi Omegas are listening with interest. Some pat their purses and hold up wallets to indicate that they're ready to go.

"Our plan is to have goods and services available in all of our shops and restaurants, and you're welcome to mosey around at your own pace and visit anywhere you like." Holly points at both sides of the streets with her fingers the way a flight attendant might point out emergency exits. "If you'd like to do any of your holiday shopping here, Cap Duncan has a variety of cigars at North Star Cigars, and the lovely Ellen and Carrie-Anne have all kinds of items for sale at Mistletoe Morning Brew."

The Omegas start to whisper and point at the different shops as Holly talks.

"Tinsel & Tidings is not just our island grocery store, but also a gift shop, so if there's something Christmas Key related that you'd like to purchase, the triplets sell all kinds of souvenirs."

"Do you have t-shirts?" asks a lady in a sun visor and shorts.

"T-shirts, handmade key chains, decorative shells, a Christmas Key calendar, postcards...the list goes on," Holly says. "And our restaurants have keepsakes for sale, too. At Jack Frosty's you can buy beer mugs or glasses with the logo on it as well as t-shirts, and at the

Jingle Bell Bistro, the Cafferkeys sell boxes of mix so that you can take home their secret recipe for Irish soda biscuits. Vance Guy has books for sale at the book store, and if you feel like getting anyone on your list a gift certificate to the Christmas Key B&B, come and see me."

"Don't forget about me!" Joe Sacamano says jovially as he walks out of Mistletoe Morning Brew with a coffee in his hand. "I'm set up at that table down there," he says, pointing at a folding table in front of Poinsettia Plaza.

"I would never forget you, Joe," Holly laughs. "Mr. Sacamano has a variety of his own homemade rum for sale down there, and he'll even box it up for you and make it safe to pack in your suitcase for travel."

"I've got coconut, lime, guava—all kinds of experimental artisan rums." Joe points again at his table with one strong, tanned arm. "So come and see me, ladies." He winks at the women from beneath a cap of snowy white curls, charming them all with his icy blue eyes and handsome face. Holly can nearly feel the women of all ages swoon a little as he struts down the street with his coffee in hand.

"There are also a couple of other tables on Main Street," Holly says, trying to draw the women's attention back. "Maggie Sutter is selling her hand-crocheted goods over there," Holly gestures at a table that's set up in front of Jack Frosty's, "and our youngest shop-keepers, Mexi and Mori, have a table full of their beach art at the end of the street if you'd like to purchase a unique piece that incorporates shells and sand from Christmas Key." The women chuckle politely as they wave at Mexi and Mori, dressed in matching shorts and Hawaiian shirts. The boys wave back from their chairs behind a table that's being manned by Idora.

"You're also welcome to pick up beauty products from Scissors & Ribbons," Holly adds. "And we have a special gift-wrapping station set up under the palm trees down at the old dock if you'd like to have our elves get everything ready to go directly under the Christmas tree." Emily Cafferkey, Heddie, and Millie Bradford—all in matching Santa hats—wave from the end of the street by the old dock when Holly points in their direction.

"After shopping and lunch, we'll meet in the dining room for cocktail hour at five o'clock so we can finally solve this murder mystery, and then we'll migrate over to the boat after that in hopes of boarding at seven so we can have you all back in Key West before it gets too late. Sound good?"

There are nods and whoops of approval from all around, so Holly waves both hands to let the crowd know that it's time to shop. Women scatter, and within minutes, Holly is standing alone on Main Street with the sun warming her still-damp hair. Buckhunter turns on a playlist of tropical Christmas music that pours from the speakers up and down Main Street, and the sound of steel drums and ukuleles playing holiday classics fills the air. Holly breathes in deeply.

"Hey, Holly," Katelynn says. She's pushing her grandfather up the sidewalk in a wheelchair. Holly walks over to talk to Hal for a few minutes. He seems aware of who she is, though he doesn't say much. Katelynn holds onto the handles of his wheelchair and gives Holly a sad look over the top of his head.

"We're just looking at what's for sale," Katelynn explains. "Grandpa wanted to get out of the house for a bit."

"I don't blame you, Hal—it's a gorgeous day."

Hal nods. His frail hands are clasped in front of him on his lap. It's amazing to Holly how rapid his decline has been.

"We're going to head over to Joe's rum stand and have a look." Katelynn adjusts the purse she's got slung across her body. "Hopefully have a sample, if he's offering any."

Holly suddenly remembers her promise to check out the space above North Star Cigars for Logan's radio station. "I'm going to grab my keys right now and have a look around at the office area I talked to Logan about. I'll let you know if it looks like it'll work or not."

"Sounds good. Thanks, Hol." Katelynn pushes her grandfather on, and as promised, Holly dashes into the B&B office and retrieves the ring of keys that open all the stores and shops up and down Main Street.

The narrow stairs in the back of the cigar shop creak as Holly steps carefully through a maze of catalog piles and little cigar boxes.

She'll have to ask Cap to clean the area up and stop using it as a storage space for things that need to be recycled.

At the top of the stairs is a door with a lock that fits an old fashioned skeleton key. Holly smiles at this charming detail, remembering how her grandpa had loved carrying around a keyring full of the long skeleton keys for all the businesses. In the years since his passing, however, she's had to change out most of the locks for stainless steel ones because the salty sea air rusted the old ones.

The door gives way with a fair amount of shoving, and Holly finds herself in the middle of a narrow space. The roof is pitched, and the dusty window that looks down onto Main Street is uncovered. She's facing north so no direct sunlight streams in, but it is bright, and a warm golden light fills the room. Holly sets the keys on a small table and steps over boxes with their flaps askew. She bends over one and peers inside.

"What is this?" She squats down and opens the first box. There are shirts inside. She pulls one out, shaking it until it unfurls and she's holding it up to the light from the window. "Christmas Key," she reads on the front, then turns it around. "What a wonderful place to be." Tears fill her eyes as she realizes that these shirts must have been the work of her grandpa in his quest to make the island into the paradise he and her grandmother always wanted it to be.

Holly paws through the box, unearthing a pile of the t-shirts in various sizes. They're the pale yellow of sunlight with a fully-colored scene on the back of a Santa Claus in sunglasses and surf trunks lounging against a palm tree. She smiles and puts the shirts back in the box.

The cardboard feels dusty in her hands as she shifts boxes around, opening another that's filled with brochures. Holly unfolds one and her mouth drops open as she sees a photo of herself standing on a totally undeveloped Main Street. She'd been a toddler when the photo was taken and her grandma had posed her in the middle of the sandy, unpaved road wearing a white summer dress and sandals. She has her little hands on her hips, and she's looking towards the camera with wide eyes. Her hair is in two pigtails tied off with ribbons.

Ever dreamed of retiring to a wild paradise? Are you full of adventure and the desire to live your dreams? Christmas Key, located in the southern Florida Keys, is an island in development. Raise your children here, or retire and spend your golden years in the sun. Contact Frank and Jeanie Baxter for more information today! Holly closes the brochure and flips it over. On the back is a phone number with a Miami area code and a P.O. Box to write to for more details. Surely the number and address were to an attorney or a real estate agent that her grandparents had used when they'd first started the journey towards developing the island. She closes the box and pushes it towards the t-shirts. She'll be taking both boxes with her.

Holly stands and walks to the window, looking down at the scene below. The windowpane is in desperate need of cleaning, but she has a clear view of the whole street, including the spot up near where Jack Frosty's now stands where her grandma had posed her for the photo on the brochure. She lets everything in her field of vision blur as she tries to remember what it was like before the shops had started to pop up and before golf carts zipped up and down the now paved street. She can hardly imagine it.

With one final look at the spot where her pigtailed toddler self had stood, Holly turns and surveys the office space. It's small, but would be perfect for Logan. It's not a storefront and no one's used it in years, so she has no need to charge rent for the space. Electricity will run through Cap's shop, and it'll be easy to see how much it jumps in the first couple of months of use and to compensate Cap for the difference so that he's not paying it out of his own pocket.

The little table where she's set her keys could be pushed over to the window, and with everything cleared out, Logan will have room to set up all of his equipment and get WXMS up and running in no time. Holly smiles at the happy jumble of items she's uncovered, kicking at another box until the flap falls open and reveals a mound of tinsel in various colors. She smiles at this because—of course—

there are more Christmas decorations packed away in an unused space. There are *always* more Christmas decorations.

Holly is about to take her two boxes with her and depart for the day when she spots a cardboard tube standing upright and leaning in the corner. She'd initially mistaken it for an empty roll of wrapping paper, but with closer inspection, she sees that it's got a lid on one end. With a little maneuvering, she loosens the white plastic lid and turns the tube so that she can peer in with one eye. There's a rolled up paper inside.

Holly holds the cylinder in one hand and puts her fingers in, feeling around for an edge of the paper to grab. When she finally has it, she carefully slides the rolled-up paper out and sets it on the table. *A poster?* she wonders, unrolling it slowly. But instead of a poster advertising paradise, it's an artist's rendering of the island from 1988 that looks like a hand-drawn map of an imaginary, faraway land created for a fantasy novel.

The outline and shape of the island are familiar, but everything is still undeveloped. There's a spot blocked off for the family's property, where Holly's and Buckhunter's houses now stand, and Main Street is drawn with little blocks of space for storefronts. The rest of the island is all trees and foliage, with winding streets that look like streams, their proposed names etched lightly next to them.

"White Christmas Way," Holly reads, tracing the street with her finger. "Cinnamon Lane. Snowflake Banks." These reminders of how far things have come—of how much the island has changed—are invigorating. Some days Holly gets so bogged down in the day to day machinations of running her island that she forgets what it means to be where she is. The amount of blood, sweat, tears, and sheer dreaming that went into turning this wild, untamed island into what it is today amazes her. Not for the first time, she thinks admiringly of her grandparents and of all that they did to make this place a reality.

Holly rolls the map up again and slides it back into the tube. She pulls out her phone and sends a text to Miguel: *I'm upstairs above the cigar shop. Need a little help carrying boxes. Can you come?* His reply is quick: *Yep. Be right there, boss!*

It isn't until she's gathered the boxes that she wants to take, and moved a few things around while she waits for Miguel that Holly is hit with a simple realization: not long ago, it would have been Jake she sent the text to asking for help. Even with River in her life, she'd always counted on Jake to be there when she needed him.

Now, for the first time in a long time, Jake hadn't even come to mind.

16

"WHAT ARE YOU DOING HERE?" HOLLY DROPS THE BOX OF T-SHIRTS onto the floor of the B&B's office. A cloud of dust rises from the cardboard and Bonnie is taken over by an exaggerated coughing fit. She waves her hand in front of her face and squints her eyes.

"Sugar, I didn't die last night—are you trying to kill me now?"

"No," Holly says, standing up straight. "But once again, what are you doing here? Didn't Fiona order you to stay in bed for the day and rest?"

Miguel has followed Holly into the office with the box of pamphlets and the tube that holds the island map in his arms. He sets both down gently and stands in the doorway.

"Honey," Bonnie stands up slowly, bracing herself against the edge of her desk. "Fiona might have *suggested* that I rest up today, but there's no rest for the wicked, and the righteous don't need none."

"So you're too righteous to follow the doctor's orders?" Holly assumes a bossy stance.

"I'm too ornery to follow doctor's orders." Bonnie walks more slowly than usual over to the boxes that Holly and Miguel have carried in. "What's all this?"

Holly isn't done with her stern look, so she stays where she is, gazing at Bonnie with narrowed eyes. Finally, she drops the disapproving squint and bends over to open one of the boxes. "I found this in the office space above North Star Cigars. It looks like stuff my grandpa ordered at one point."

"Would you look at this!" Bonnie hoots, pulling a out pamphlet and holding it up. "You're knee-high to a grasshopper in this picture. Look at you, baby girl!" Her eyes well up with tears as she looks at Holly in her sundress and pigtails. "This is too, too precious."

Miguel leans in close and looks at the photo. "Is this you?" he asks Holly. He peers out the window. "On Main Street?"

"Indeed it is," Holly says. "Can you believe how much it's all changed?"

"I can. But what I can't believe is how cute you were," Miguel looks at the pamphlet again and then back at Holly. "What happened?"

Holly gives him a light punch on the arm. As her knuckles connect with his firm bicep, she can feel the strength honed through doing construction work under the hot sun.

"Ouch," Miguel says mildly, though the punch was so light that it couldn't have hurt at all.

"But there's more." Holly opens the other box and takes out two of the yellow shirts. "I have these in various sizes." She tosses the shirts at Bonnie and Miguel, who unfold them and admire both front and back.

"Totally retro," says Miguel.

"I'll be damned," says Bonnie.

"But my very favorite thing is this." Holly pulls the lid off the poster tube again and slides the map out carefully. She hands one end to Miguel to hold and then unrolls it slowly, revealing the map for them to see. Bonnie gives a low whistle. "I want to get this framed," Holly says. "I think it belongs here at the B&B somewhere. Either in the office or out front."

"It's too cool to hide," Bonnie says. "I think you should put it in the lobby."

"Maybe scan it and use the map on other things. Like a new brochure. Or your website," Miguel offers.

Holly nods, turning both suggestions over in her mind. She isn't sure yet what she'll do with the shirts and brochures, but the map will definitely be something she shows off or uses in some way. She rolls her end towards Miguel's and then slides the map back into its tube.

"Anyway, this is stuff we can work on later, but I wanted to bring it over since I was up in the office poking around."

"What made you go up there? I don't think I've ever even set foot behind the front counter of Cap's shop." Bonnie sits in her chair again. She still looks a little tired from the night before, but Holly watches her closely, noting that beyond the weariness, nothing else seems to be terribly amiss.

"Logan wants to start a radio station here on the island using his great-grandpa's old equipment—"

"You mean all that stuff you used to spend hours messing around with, listening to that heavy metal music from people in other states?"

"Bon, The Cure isn't heavy metal," Holly says patiently, feeling like she's explaining basic technology to her elderly aunt or something.

"What's The Cure?" Miguel frowns.

Holly looks back and forth between them with blatant shock. "The two of you must be educated. Immediately." She pushes the box of t-shirts out of the way with the toe of her Converse. "Let me fix this." She bends over her computer and pushes the power button, bringing it to life. With a few quick strokes, she's logged into Spotify and pulled up one of her favorite playlists. "Bon, I play this some-times. You'll know this song."

The opening notes of "Friday I'm in Love" fill the room.

"Ohhhhh," Bonnie nods. "Okay, I know this one. This isn't heavy metal."

"I've heard this." Miguel listens to the song.

"Okay, thank God," Holly says with relief. "Now I can move on with my day feeling like I've done a good deed. Miguel, you officially know a Cure song," she says, moving her mouse and choosing another playlist. "And Bonnie, FYI, *this* is metal." She clicks on a song and Metallica's "Enter Sandman" starts to play.

Bonnie covers her ears and shakes her head. "I think I like The Cure better."

"That's my girl." Holly closes the laptop and the music stops. "Okay, let's get a move on here. We've got—" Holly looks at her watch —"about two and a half hours until we're supposed to convene in the dining room for cocktail hour. And we have no idea who killed Santa or the elf. I'm totally at a loss on that one."

"I think Mrs. Claus knows more than she's letting on," Bonnie says sagely. Her lips are pursed as she nods at Holly and Miguel. "There's something not quite right about her."

"I think Mrs. Claus is just a nice old lady—no offense," Miguel says, looking at Bonnie quickly to make sure he hasn't offended.

"None taken, honeybun. I don't consider myself old." Bonnie pats her red hair and sniffs almost imperceptibly, though Holly picks up on it.

"I don't know. There've been so many red herrings that I got lost along the way. I wonder if any of the Alpha Chi Omegas have been able to work through all the clues."

Bonnie pushes herself out of the chair again. "I'm sure some of those busybodies have come up with an answer or two. Now, sugar, would you mind dropping me home before this big cocktail party? I feel like I could rest again."

Holly rushes to Bonnie's side and offers her an arm. "Yeah, of course. Let's get you home for a nap." They leave the office with Miguel behind them. "I need to run home and change anyway, so I'll swing back by and get you before cocktail hour, as long as you feel up to it."

"I'll feel up to it, doll. I'm tough as a pine knot. I just need a quick little bit of shut eye, and then I'm good to go."

※

HOLLY KICKS OFF HER SHOES AT THE FRONT DOOR AND WANDERS through her house. There's a pile of magazines and unopened mail on her kitchen table that needs attention, so she gathers it all and takes it out onto the lanai with a can of 7Up. Pucci follows, his body swaying from side to side as he ambles out after her.

Power bill. Letter from some attorney or something in Savannah. Bathing suit catalog. B&B mail that accidentally got mixed into the pile. Holly sorts through everything, sifting out the junk mail that she can automatically recycle. Before opening anything, she cracks open her can of soda and sits back, putting her bare feet up on one of the other chairs.

It's sunny and the trees are waving languidly in the afternoon breeze. Across the small expanse of sandy grass sits Buckhunter and Fiona's bungalow. Their kitchen window is dark, and there are no carts parked in front of the house, so Holly knows they're both gone.

Having Fiona right next door since the wedding has been nice— the women often sit on the lanai and chat in the evenings, and they've had dinner together more often when Buckhunter is still at Jack Frosty's. There was a time not long ago that Holly thought of Buckhunter as annoying and it really put her out to have someone she didn't think of as family living on her property, but once she found out the truth about their relation, her whole outlook had shifted. She and Buckhunter are family, and finding out that she had an uncle living right next door has brought her nothing but happiness.

The crunch of tires on shells pulls Holly out of her thoughts and she leans forward in her chair to see Fiona pulling up in her golf cart.

"Hey." Fiona turns off the cart and leaves it in the grass between the two bungalows. "You ready for this cocktail party to happen and for this weekend to wind down?" She walks up to the screened lanai and looks in. "I heard there'll be booze."

"There will definitely be adult beverages on hand," Holly says, lifting her can of 7Up. "Wanna come in for a few?"

Fiona looks at the Apple Watch on her wrist. "Can't. I just stopped at home to grab my phone charger, and I need to get over to the B&B and check on one of our guests."

"What happened?" Holly is up and on her feet before she's even done asking the question.

"Nothing major. Sit, sit," Fiona says, holding out a hand to calm her friend. "I think she just has an ovarian cyst, but she's in a fair amount of pain so I want to do a quick ultrasound in the office and give her some ibuprofen until she can get home and see her regular doctor. No big deal."

Holly relaxes. Fiona has everything under control, and as long as there are no dead bodies—real or otherwise—and no one is bleeding or drowning, Holly is going to let her handle it. "Okay. I need to get ready and go pick Bonnie up anyway."

"Has she been resting at home all day?" Fiona asks hopefully.

Holly gives her a look from beneath raised eyebrows. "Can you really imagine Bonnie sitting around her house all day and missing out on whatever is going on around the island?"

"Good point." Fiona wags a finger at Holly. "Can you make sure she doesn't overdo it, though? I think you're the only one she'll listen to."

"Not to worry, Doc. I have everything under control."

17

THE DINING ROOM IS ONCE AGAIN LIT UP LIKE MACY'S AT Christmastime. Lights twinkle from every corner of the room, and tinsel glitters from the tree and hangs over the doors and on the bar. An upbeat, contemporary mix of holiday favorites is playing, and the room is full of Alpha Chi Omegas in sundresses and lipstick.

There are piles and piles of luggage and gifts purchased that day all wrapped in Christmas paper sitting in the lobby, and everything is tagged and ready for Cap, Wyatt, and Jimmy Cafferkey to quickly transport to the boat at the new dock so that their guests can migrate over to the vessel as soon as the cocktail party ends.

Holly moves through the room, smiling at people and stopping to talk about the things they've purchased on the island to take home for friends and family. She's pleased with how many of them seem to love Joe's homemade rum and the cute artwork that Mexi and Mori had for sale, and there's a tangible feeling of excitement as the women share last minute thoughts about the murder mystery.

"You look nice," Jake says, walking up to Holly. "I always liked you in red."

"You'd better make sure your lady doesn't catch you complimenting another woman like that." Holly pinches his arm. She's wearing a clingy, long-sleeved, red wrap dress that ties at the waist, and a pair of low-heeled sandals. It felt festive enough for cocktails and like an appropriate way to see her guests off the island.

"Who, Katelynn?" Jake makes an innocent face.

Holly wants to tease back, but for some reason, she's not really in the mood. "Yeah, Katelynn," she says softly. "You two seem happy together."

Jake gives Holly a long look. He's assessing her tone and he decides to match her level of seriousness. "I really like Katelynn," he says, keeping his eyes on Holly's. "Things are going well."

"Good. I want that for you." Holly holds his gaze, refusing to look away first. "Last Christmas" by Wham! starts playing on the speakers.

"One of your favorite Christmas songs," Jake says, pointing a finger into the air.

"One of my all-time favorites," Holly agrees. "Like an old pair of jeans that always feels right."

"Old jeans that always feel right are amazing." Jake smiles at Holly. "Just like good friends who only want the best for you."

Katelynn appears in the doorway of the dining room, looking around eagerly for Jake.

"I think you're wanted." Holly nods in Katelynn's direction. "And good luck solving the murder mystery," she adds. "I have no clue whodunnit or why, so I just want someone to make a good guess and figure this thing out."

"Same," Jake says. "I stopped trying to figure it out after Mrs. Claus got caught with her hand in the cookie jar."

Holly folds her arms across her chest and watches Jake as he cuts a path through the room to meet Katelynn. They really do look happy together, and—to her surprise—Holly feels no jealousy as she watches them embrace.

"We should just leave all these decorations up and do Christmas Eve right here," Bonnie says when she materializes at Holly's side. "Get everyone to sign up for a potluck dish and have Cap dress up like Santa."

"You think you'll still be here on Christmas Eve, or are you planning on jumping ship with Jantzen?"

Bonnie shoots Holly a look.

"Sorry, too soon?"

"Maybe for a jumping ship joke..."

Holly slings an arm around Bonnie's shoulders. "I'm just teasing—you know I am. But speaking of our favorite mystery author, where is he?"

"He dropped by my place this afternoon to check on me," Bonnie says. "He's really something else, sugar."

In Holly's opinion, this remains to be seen, but she's willing to take Bonnie's word for it because she seems so smitten with Jantzen Parks.

"Ladies." As if summoned, Jantzen walks up to Holly and Bonnie. He leans forward and plants a chaste kiss on Bonnie's cheek under Holly's watchful eye. "This has been quite a weekend," he says to Holly. "I give a lot of readings, but I don't know if I've ever had this much fun or excitement."

Holly works hard to keep her face from giving her away, because on the inside she's dying to give Jantzen Parks a piece of her mind on what exactly constitutes "fun" and "excitement." Instead, she smiles placidly and says, "Oh, good. I'm so glad you've enjoyed Christmas Key."

"I really have. In fact, I've enjoyed it so much that I'm curious to find out more about how a person might buy a little shack here for the winter." He winks at Bonnie. Holly nearly chokes.

"Jantzen! I had no idea you were thinking of even visiting us again." Bonnie bats her eyelashes at him, looking more like her old self than she has all day.

"I could hole up here for the winter and just write," he says. "It would be perfect. Far from civilization. No distractions."

Bonnie blinks again rapidly—this time in surprise. Holly knows that Bonnie considers herself a major distraction, and she's clearly disappointed that Jantzen doesn't think the same. But she rallies and plasters a pleased smile on her face.

"Well, we'd be lucky to have you," Bonnie says. When Holly stays quiet, Bonnie elbows her. "Wouldn't we, Mayor?"

"That would be a first," Holly says, jumping back into the conversation. "We've never had a famous author living in our midst before."

"How about when I get back to my home base, I give you a call. I'd like to talk more about it."

"Sure," Holly says. "Give us a call." She's already on shaky ground because of Bonnie's near miss the night before, so imagining her spending the winters shacking up with Jantzen Parks somewhere on the island (or, God forbid, following him off the island for the rest of the year) doesn't sit well with her.

Hamlet and Margo are standing near the bar, so Holly excuses herself and leaves Bonnie and Jantzen talking in the center of the dining room.

"Holly!" Margo beams at her. "Bonnie looks fabulous. Like nothing happened at all."

"And she's already back and flirting with that author fellow," Hamlet says admiringly. "Gotta give it to her—that gal's got gumption."

"That she does." Holly takes a step towards the bar and reaches for a glass of the champagne that Buckhunter has poured and set on a tray. "Now, about this murder mystery," she says.

"No, ma'am." Margo shakes her head. "We're not giving you a final clue or helping you to solve this thing."

"You won't even answer a few yes or no questions?" Holly prods. She takes a sip of her champagne and the bubbles tickle her nose and throat.

"Not a single one." Hamlet's eyes twinkle. "Even for a gorgeous mayor with gams that would've given Cyd Charisse a run for her money." He lets his eyes graze Holly's bare legs.

"Oh, for the love of crime and Christmas," Margo says, turning to face her husband with a look of amused annoyance.

Holly tries not to laugh at Margo's theme-appropriate exclamation. She'll have to pocket "for the love of crime and Christmas" for later use.

"I guess this would be a good time for me to get everyone's attention," Holly says. She drains her champagne flute and sets it on the bar. "I'll just say my part and then you two can come up and do the rest, okay?"

"We're right on your heels, doll," Hamlet says. He puts one hand on the small of his wife's back and waits for Holly to get everyone's attention.

"Good evening," Holly says from behind the podium that she uses for the monthly village council meetings. There's no need for a microphone, but she signals to Jake to cut the music so she can be heard over the noise and chatter. "Thank you all for a wonderful weekend," she says once the talking has died down. "This has been a first for us, and we've all enjoyed having you here with us on Christmas Key."

The Alpha Chi Omegas pull out chairs and sit down with their drinks as Holly talks, and the locals do the same, mixing in at the round tables and setting their glasses of champagne or cocktails on the freshly-ironed red and green plaid tablecloths. As Holly looks out at the dining room, she has a brief memory of the first year the B&B opened, and of the little tree she'd set up in one corner for the holidays. She'd invited everyone to join her there, and to her amazement, the whole island had turned up with drinks and hot dishes in hand, and just like that, their Christmas tradition had been born.

"Having a weekend full of mystery and intrigue has been fun for us, and we hope you've enjoyed it as much as we have," she says, scanning the room as she speaks. "Now, I'd like to hand you over to Hamlet and Margo so that we can finally get these murders *solved*!"

There's chatter and applause as Hamlet walks his wife over to the podium. Holly takes a step back and lets Hamlet speak.

"We've watched you all sleuthing and digging for clues this weekend, and it's been amazing for us to be able to do this in a tropical paradise," he says. "But even in paradise, bad things can happen. And they have." His tone grows dark as he lowers his voice. "We've lost a gorgeous young elf in the prime of her life. And we've lost Santa Claus."

"These are horrible, unspeakable crimes," Margo says. Her eyes dart around the room. "In the span of one evening, a young lady over-dosed and Santa Claus collapsed in this dining room and came to an untimely demise. We need to find out what happened, and at least one of you has the answer. Who at this party knows what *really* happened the other night?"

Plastic Surgery Lady stands up at her table (Holly mentally kicks herself for continuing to think of the woman that way, but she can't help it).

"I think I know exactly what went down here," she says, smoothing the fabric of an expensive looking cream and gold striped silk dress over her hips. "My friends and I have examined the facts closely, and we've come to the conclusion that Santa and his elf were in the throes of an affair. They'd been carrying on for months and hoping not to get caught, but Mrs. Claus got wind of it and she wasn't happy."

Around the room, heads swivel and all eyes turn to the woman speaking. Some people have glasses in hand, and others are consulting notepads on their tables or whispering to the person next to them.

Another woman at the table stands and speaks. "After Mrs. Claus found out, we think she told Nigel Winters, who had always secretly been in love with Mrs. Claus. He saw an opening and decided to get rid of Santa, but he didn't count on running into the floozy who'd stolen Santa's heart in the kitchen of the B&B as he created a deadly mix intended for Santa."

People are nodding and frowning intently around the room. A hand goes up at another table, but the speaker ignores it for the moment. "When he saw the elf—and, more importantly, when the elf saw him—he knew he had to kill her, too. So he followed her down the hall and watched her knock on the door of Jantzen Parks— mystery author, known lothario, and Nigel Winters' best friend since college."

A collective gasp travels around the room and everyone turns in Jantzen's direction. He sits at a table next to Bonnie, his face a mask of shock and innocence. "Me?" he says. "I know nothing about a dead elf. I wasn't even there, was I?" Jantzen looks at Bonnie pleadingly. "I was...otherwise engaged that evening," he says delicately. "And I have someone who can vouch for me."

"You have an alibi?" Hamlet demands.

"I do. I was with Bonnie Lane all evening."

Another gasp. A woman near Holly whispers, "Now *that's* the real floozy."

"This is all very intriguing," Hamlet says, pulling everyone's attention back. He runs a hand over his white goatee and puzzles over this explanation. "You have some very good ideas and you've clearly done your research. Impressive."

"But incorrect," says Cap, standing up at the table he's sharing with Heddie and the triplets and their husbands. "We know what really happened."

"Oh, you do?" Margo asks with a look of interest. "Please, do tell."

"Here's what we know," Cap says. "We know that an elf died. We know Santa dropped here in the dining room. And we know that Mrs. Claus got caught kissing Santa's business manager the very next day. But we don't know whether any of this was as shocking to the main players as it was to all of us. We think Santa and Mrs. Claus had an arrangement of sorts."

"An arrangement?" Margo prompts.

"You know," Cap says, "an arrangement—an open type of marriage. You see who you want, I'll see who I want, just keep it quiet so that people don't talk. Don't tarnish Santa's good name. They're just humans, too."

"Interesting," Hamlet says. He's got his arms folded over his chest. "Go on."

"So Santa is having his fun with a cute little elf, but things get out of hand. Maybe she's taken some pills or something and she hits her head. She's unconscious and he knows he can't have a dead elf on his hands. So he corners Jantzen Parks and begs him to help. And really, who among us could say no to Santa? So Jantzen helps him move the body into his hotel room and he escapes out the window and runs to Bonnie to hide him."

People glance at Jantzen and Bonnie again as if they're on trial. They huddle close together.

"After Jantzen is gone and the elf is discovered, the shock of it all hits Santa unexpectedly, and bing, bang, boom—he dies of a heart attack. Now Mrs. Claus and Nigel Winters are free to carry on, as they've already been doing for years."

"A very, very, very good guess," Hamlet says, clapping his hands together in a solo round of applause. "But we're not there yet."

The room is silent as everyone waits on pins and needles for more. Lights twinkle and the candles in their hurricane lamps on each table flicker warmly, casting light on the red and green centerpieces made of holly and pinecones.

"Does anyone else have a—" Margo says, hands clasped in front of her.

But as she's speaking, the doors to the dining room fly open. Yet another wave of shock goes through the crowd. There, dressed from head to toe in red and white, black boots polished to a high shine, stands Santa.

"I have an explanation," he says in his booming voice. "And it involves *her*."

Holly realizes just a beat after everyone else that Santa's white-gloved finger is pointing directly at her.

18

"Holly Jean Baxter," Bonnie says loudly. "Did you kill Santa, young lady?"

Holly's mouth is still open and her heart is fluttering in her chest. "He's not dead. He's right there," she says dumbly, pointing back at Santa.

"Nobody killed anybody," Santa says. He walks across the room slowly, leading with his large, protruding belly. He makes his way through the tables towards Holly, and each person in the room follows him with their eyes as he passes. "My beloved elf made some poor choices about men and fell in with a scoundrel," he says, stopping in the middle of the dining room to turn and look sternly at Jantzen Parks. "She followed her heart all the way down a bottle of pills and things ended badly for her. I've known for months that she'd been carrying on with this mystery author and that they were planning to meet up here on Christmas Key, but I had no idea his intentions with her were this dark."

"It was an accident!" Jantzen pounds the table with both fists and pushes his chair back as he stands. His face is red and angry, and there is a storm brewing behind his eyes as he fumes. "She threatened to hurt herself if I didn't marry her, but I thought we were just having fun." He jabs a finger in Santa's direction for emphasis.

"Playing with someone's heart is never fun," Santa says with a grave tone. He glares at Jantzen from under his thick, white brows. "Regardless of whether she meant to harm herself or not, a lovely young elf is gone, and you, Jantzen Parks, are to blame."

Holly's eyes dart around the room as she takes in the shocked faces. It's as if everyone in the room is spellbound. Mouths are open, eyes are wide. Everyone waits for the next bombshell.

"Now, as for me," Santa says, resuming his slow walk towards Holly. "I have to admit that I faked my own death."

"What?" Maria Agnelli shouts out into the silent room.

"He said he faked his own death," Millie whispers to her loudly.

Mrs. Agnelli waves a hand and makes a disgusted face. "Sweet fancy Moses," she says, "what a load of—"

Santa cuts her off. "I got wind of a devious plan cooked up by none other than my own business manager, Mr. Nigel Winters. Not only did he introduce my sweet, young elf to his college buddy Jantzen Parks, but he had his sights set on taking my place."

A hush fills the room as Santa steps up to his throne and turns to face the whole crowd. "Simply stated," Santa says, lowering himself into the tall chair by putting a hand on one knee, "Nigel Winters wanted to be Santa Claus."

Mrs. Claus puts both hands over her mouth as she watches her husband who—until just minutes ago—she thought was dead.

"He used you, Carol," Santa says sadly, looking at his wife. "He flirted with you mercilessly and was ready to fill my boots. To sit on my throne. To *drive my sleigh*," he adds with emphasis.

"I did no such thing," Nigel says with conviction.

"You did," Santa argues calmly. "You planned on poisoning me, just like that lady guessed. But she wasn't the only one to figure it out. I knew it and decided to beat you to the punch by having a heart attack and disappearing. And what did you do? Moved in on my wife the very next day."

"But—" Nigel pleads.

Santa holds up both gloved hands. "No need to explain, Nigel. It didn't work and it never would have. Carol and I may not be perfect, but she makes all my days merry and bright." He motions for his wife, who stands and walks over to his side.

"I'm so happy that you're alive," Mrs. Claus says to her husband. "But what does all of this have to do with her?" She turns and looks at Holly.

"With Holly?" Santa says softly. There's a twinkle in his eye as he holds his wife close with one arm. "Well, when Holly was a little girl, she wrote a letter to Santa one year asking him if he knew where Christmas Key was."

Holly's smile fades and a chill runs up her spine.

"She asked him if he'd ever consider coming to the island with Mrs. Claus to check it out and see if they might want to live here full time. Do you remember that, Holly?"

Her eyes are filled with tears as she recalls the letter she'd written at her grandmother's suggestion. She nods at Santa. "I remember."

"So we had to come and check it out. And let me tell you, Christmas Key is a magical place, but the North Pole is home." He smiles at Holly kindly. "Besides, there's not enough room on this island for all my elves and reindeer!"

Laughter breaks out around the room and Holly joins in, swiping at a stray tear that's escaped from one eye. There is applause from around the room and lots of talking as people discuss the outcome of the mystery. The formerly deceased elf walks in through the doors of the dining room to more applause, and it takes a moment for Holly to adjust to the fact that the people standing at the front of the room aren't *really* Santa and Mrs. Claus and that both Santa and the elf are really alive and well.

She looks over at Bonnie and Jantzen and tries to see him with new eyes. Was he playing a role, too? Is he really a heartbreaker who doesn't care about Bonnie, or is he actually a best-selling author who just happened to get roped into playing along with the murder mystery this weekend? It'll take her a moment to sort it all out in her mind.

"I hope we didn't throw you off too much by including you in this bit here," Santa says, walking towards Holly with outstretched arms. He takes her hands in his gloved ones. "It really was a sweet letter, young lady. Santa and Mrs. Claus should be honored to be invited to live on Christmas Key."

Holly feels a flush creeping up her neck. "But...how did you know about that?" she asks, looking back and forth between Santa and Mrs. Claus as they stand in front of her.

"Oh, honey," Mrs. Claus says. She's holding her hands in front of her rounded stomach. "Santa knows everything."

They look at each other lovingly and Santa gives Holly's hands a squeeze before they walk away. She still has no clue how they would have known the contents of that letter.

"Hamlet! Margo!" Holly calls out, walking after the older couple as they make their way to the bar. "I have to ask you something."

"Mayor, you can ask us anything you like now that the mystery has been solved." Margo smiles at Holly.

"It's about Jantzen Parks," she says, lowering her voice. "What does he really have to do with all of this?"

Margo gives Hamlet a look. "Nothing. We just met him on the first night and thought he might want to play along. He's been a good sport."

"So, that bit about him and the elf..." Holly narrows her eyes.

"Just that," Hamlet says, turning his palms to the ceiling. "A bit. Nothing more. He seems like a very nice guy."

Holly smiles at Hamlet and Margo and excuses herself. So Jantzen really *is* just a mystery author and not a traveling lothario with devious plans to lure unsuspecting women into his lair. He did, however, get Bonnie onto a boat and into a dangerous situation, and for that she won't easily forgive him. But maybe, just maybe, he's a decent guy who really likes Bonnie as much as she likes him.

"So, we failed." Miguel says as he and Fiona join Holly. "I thought we'd at least come up with a viable solution to pitch tonight."

"Well, I couldn't really pitch in too many ideas since I was privy to all the behind-the-scenes stuff with Santa and the elf," Fiona points out.

"True..." Holly is distracted as she surveys the room. The Alpha Chi Omegas all seem satisfied with the outcome of the mystery and are enjoying their final glasses of wine and champagne before heading back to the boat. "To be perfectly honest though, I got really distracted by everything else that was going on here. Between Mrs. Agnelli and Idora's shouting match, and having to stay on top of the B&B and the events we'd planned for everyone this weekend, I kept forgetting that we had a mystery to solve."

"I'm sure it works better if you're on vacation," Miguel says. "You get lost in the details and you really believe the actors more."

Holly looks at Fiona and Miguel guiltily. "Okay, I actually did buy into the actors more than I should have. Like, I'm standing here now still thinking that Santa Claus is in the room with us. And the fact that she's alive," Holly says, gesturing at the elf, who is laughing and chatting with Jake and Katelynn, "that really weirds me out."

"Awww, he really got you with that letter, huh?" Fiona puts her arm around Holly. "Do you actually remember writing that?"

"I do," Holly says, feeling the tears threaten the back of her eyes again. "I wanted to know if Santa would find Christmas Key since I was the only kid here—this was before Iris and Jimmy moved here with Emily—and my grandma told me I should write him a letter and ask. So I told him to just move down here. I figured, hey, there were other people with white hair already living here, so he and Mrs. Claus might as well just join them."

Miguel laughs out loud. "That's so cute."

"Yeah," Holly chuckles. "It is. But I still don't know how he would have known what was in that letter."

"Hey, sugar," Bonnie says, approaching the little group with Jantzen in tow. "We pulled this weekend off and I think it was a roaring success."

Holly puts both arms around Bonnie's neck and hugs her. "I think so, too." As they embrace, she eyes Jantzen cautiously. She's slowly accepting the fact that he was mostly just playing along with Hamlet and Margo's request to participate in the murder mystery, but she's not ready to throw her support behind him entirely.

"Hey, Bon. Do you know anything about that letter that Santa mentioned?"

Bonnie gives Holly a final squeeze and takes a step back to look at her. Her eyes are warm and loving. "Check your stocking, sugar."

"My stocking?"

"The one in the lobby," Bonnie says. "I found it in a file of your grandpa's in the spring and I've been hanging onto it so I could give it to you for Christmas. But when Santa showed up, I couldn't resist sharing it with him."

Holly wants to see the letter so badly that she doesn't even say anything to the group before walking straight through the dining room and into the darkened lobby. A lamp burns on the front desk and behind it hang the homemade stockings that she and Bonnie put up every year. Anyone on the island who wants their stocking hung in the B&B has added their own to the collection, and Holly scans the various shapes and sizes of stockings, looking for the hand-knit holiday sock with her name on it that Maggie Sutter made for her several years back.

From the dining room comes the strains of a tropical, instrumental version of "Frosty the Snowman." Holly stands on her tiptoes and pulls her stocking off the hook. Sure enough, an envelope rests inside. The letter is twenty-five years old and written on a sheet of white paper in a loopy, childlike hand.

Dear Santa, it says. *Can you please move to Christmas Key? It's really pretty here. I love Christmas and so does my grandma. Please bring Mrs. Claus and live here forever. I love you. Holly Baxter.*

The t-shirts and brochures she's unearthed, the map of the island, the letter...all of these memories are flooding through Holly's veins at the same time. She always misses her grandparents, but as she stands there behind the front desk of the lobby holding a letter full of childish hope and excitement, a huge pang of longing fills her heart. If she could just hold them both one more time. Or have her grandpa around to talk with about island business. If she could only sit with her grandma on the lanai, laughing and feeling like there was someone to look after her again...she misses that. She misses *them*.

With a final look at her words to Santa, Holly folds the letter and slips it back inside her stocking. She presses a hand against the knit sock lovingly, then turns back to face the pile of luggage and packages that need to be transported through the dark evening and delivered to the boat. The murder mystery weekend has been a success, but now she's got work to do.

19

"OH, I MISS HIM ALREADY," BONNIE MOPES THE NEXT MORNING. SHE'S sitting on her side of the desk at the B&B, chin resting on her fist as she gazes out the window at Main Street. Since they're only a week away from Christmas, they've got a mix of holiday music playing in the office non-stop.

Holly's fingers stop tapping at her keyboard and she looks at Bonnie. "Woman. You've only known him for four days. Everything is going to be fine."

"But sugar, you don't understand! Or maybe you do. Remember River? You went gaga over him."

Holly lets her hands fall into her lap. "Of course I remember. I've been swept off my feet before, I guess I'm just more cautious now."

"Well, don't be too cautious, or love will pass you by." Bonnie turns her attention back to the work at hand and pulls a folder from the wire basket on the corner of her desk. She looks good for being less than forty-eight hours beyond her Coast Guard rescue, but Holly still watches her closely as she flips through the papers in her file and picks out the one she needs.

Holly says nothing. She knows Bonnie is only dispensing the kind of advice that a woman who loves to be in love believes in her heart, but in Holly's mind, there's no such thing as being too cautious when it comes to matters of the heart. It's far too easy to make the kind of mistakes that, at best, haunt your dreams, and, at worst, leave you devastated.

"What do you think of trying to get more of these t-shirts made and setting up an online shop?" Holly leans over and pulls one of the yellow shirts from the box next to her desk. "I really like this design." She turns it around so that Bonnie can look at the colorful scene on the back again. "And I bet we could find someone to recreate it and make more shirts."

"Our first murder mystery weekend ended last night, and you woke up bored this morning and looking for a new challenge?" Bonnie picks up her latte and takes a sip.

"Something like that." Holly drops the shirt back into the box and opens her browser to search for companies that could make more shirts for her. She woke up early thinking about the success of the shopping event she'd put together the day before, and she's been considering the handmade items that the islanders make and how they might be able to both sell those items and advertise the island at the same time.

"I thought maybe we could sell shirts and locally made crafts. And I talked to Joe a long time ago about selling his rum online."

Bonnie sets her coffee on her coaster and leans her elbows on the desk. "Okay, I see your idea." She nods and rubs her red lips together, smacking them twice for good measure. "Stuff like Maggie's crafts and Logan's photographs of the island."

"Exactly!" Holly slaps a palm on the desk. "I even thought of that —we could use some of Logan's photos and make postcards or posters, if he's okay with that."

"I've gotta hand it to you, girl, you never do rest on your laurels."

"I'm sure that's genetic." Holly has been thinking lately of her grandpa's island prospectus, a book she used to consult far more frequently while she considered ways to make the island viable as she developed it. Frank Baxter's ideas and plans for Christmas Key had been grand, but always started with a grassroots approach to people and commerce. "I just feel like we're at a place where I need to start scaling up again. We've had tourists and groups come to the island now, we've been the backdrop for a reality show, and we've opened a few new businesses and gained some new residents. So what's next?"

"Speaking of new residents, I was thinking that Jantzen might want to see that empty house just down the street from mine."

"Sounds convenient." Holly looks at her computer screen to keep herself from laughing out loud.

"Just a thought," Bonnie says defensively. "And you're right—it is time for you to think about what comes next with this island. I know you're cooking something up as we speak. That brain has no off switch, sugar."

Holly taps the end of her pen against her front teeth as she thinks. "I have some ideas."

"Why don't you look into the website thing? I bet Logan is computer savvy enough to help you get that up and running. You know how kids are."

Holly smiles to herself. She's computer savvy enough herself to make a website, but Bonnie is right—she will need some assistance running it.

"Logan's going to be pretty busy with the radio station if we can get that going," she says. "And to be perfectly honest, I'm excited about that. It's something I wouldn't have thought of on my own, and I think people will really like it."

"Holly?" A tentative knock on the door to the office pulls both women's attention away from their conversation.

"Well, speak of the devil!" Bonnie says, smiling widely at Logan Pillory. "We were just talking about your radio station."

Logan runs a hand over his recently shorn head. His skin has gotten past the stage where he sported a constant burn from being in the tropical sun. It's turned a nice shade of tan, and his hair is flecked with golden highlights after several months on Christmas Key.

"I wanted to talk to you about that," Logan says to Holly.

"Come in." Holly stands up and grabs a chair from the corner of the room, dragging it across the office and parking it next to her own seat. "Sit."

Logan does as he's told, perching on the edge of the chair with his elbows on both knees. The morning sunlight glints off the tinsel and decorations all over Main Street, casting colorful shafts of light around the office.

"I wanted to get some of my great-grandpa's stuff moved into that office space and start setting things up," Logan says.

"I just went in there yesterday and moved a few things out." Holly leans back in her chair and stretches her legs under the desk. She's kicked off her flip-flops and she flexes her toes as she thinks. "I could probably get the rest of it moved out today at some point and then we could go in and clean it up a bit."

"I can do that," Logan offers quickly. "I can clean."

Holly smiles at his eagerness. "Okay, that would be helpful. I think the spot itself is going to be perfect, but what else do you need to do in order to get WXMS up and running?"

"I've started filling out the online forms for the FCC to apply for an operational license," Logan says. "I have to decide whether I want to run a commercial or noncommercial station before I can go any further."

"Oh, this sounds official," Bonnie says. "And exciting."

"I'm not sure which one to do. Do you think any of the businesses on the island will want to advertise? Or any other businesses?" Logan looks at Holly for advice.

"I'm not sure." Holly wiggles her toes under the desk. "I mean, it's a possibility, but at this point, I'm looking at this as more of a fun hobby with potential. Maybe you can ask a few more questions of the FCC before you file any applications or forms?"

Logan nods. "That's what I was thinking. I still really want to set things up while I'm waiting, though. I want to be ready to go when they approve me."

Holly smiles at his youthful enthusiasm. She knows the feeling well—it's the same excited sensation that makes her spine tingle every time she comes up with a new idea for the island.

"Speaking of new ventures," Holly says, sitting upright and pulling her feet underneath her thighs so that she's sitting criss-cross on her chair. "I was thinking of building a website for the island so that we can sell some of our locally made items and Christmas Key memorabilia."

Logan nods. "Sounds cool."

"In the midst of school work and radio station stuff, do you think you might want to help me get that off the ground? I can scrape together some funds and pay you," Holly offers.

Logan thinks for a second. "The website thing will be easy," he decides. "How about you let me work on that in exchange for rent on the space above the cigar shop?"

Holly nods appreciatively. "A true businessman. I knew from almost the moment we met that we had something big in common."

"I have lots of ideas," Logan says. "Just like you."

"Then let's do some business," Holly decides. She sticks a hand out for Logan to shake. "Website work in exchange for radio station rent. I like it." Logan takes her hand and shakes it firmly.

"I'll keep working on the application," Logan says.

"And I'll get everything out of the space sometime today and text you when it's free for you to start setting up."

"Deal." Logan stands up with a huge grin on his face. He picks up the chair and moves it back to the corner of the small office space. "Talk to you later."

"Bye, Logan," Bonnie says, watching him go. "Sweet kid," she says to Holly. "And a real head for business. You need to hire him to replace me when I retire." She picks up her reading glasses from the desk and slips them on, peering at the computer screen over the top of her frames.

"You're not allowed to retire." Holly reaches for a notepad and a pen as if this ends the discussion. "And by the way," she says, doodling on the paper absentmindedly, "thank you for saving my letter to Santa. That meant a lot to me."

Bonnie takes her reading glasses off and reaches across the shared desk space to grab Holly's hand. "Sugar," she says quietly. "*You* mean a lot to me. And I'm not retiring or leaving the island anytime soon, so don't you worry for even one second, you hear?"

"I hear, Bon," Holly says. "I hear."

20

LATER THAT EVENING, HOLLY IS CURLED UP ON THE COUCH, WATCHING the lights of her own Christmas tree flicker in the corner as she holds the book Bonnie has given her in her lap. She's changed into sweats and taken out her contacts.

"Come here, boy," she says, making a noise to call Pucci to her side. He ambles over and circles around on the rug in front of the couch, finally settling in near her peacefully.

There's a sense of relief for Holly each time she successfully finishes an event on the island and a group of visitors leave; it's like a return to normalcy, and she loves the feeling of knowing that while she's attempted something new and completed her mission, she can relax among the people she considers family and friends and get on with her regular life. It's a feeling that leaves her conflicted, as she's the main force behind developing the island and encouraging her neighbors to welcome new additions. Of course there are growing pains to every endeavor, and being open to change is a journey.

The house is quiet for once—she's opted not to put on any music as she reads. With a tug on the blue blanket that hangs over the back of her couch, Holly covers herself and cracks the book that Bonnie's Uncle Jack wrote about Aunt Mildred.

The look in her eyes was at once playful and a challenge; was I up to the task of bringing a woman more than three decades my senior to her knees? Did I have what it would take to keep her interested day after day, year after year? I imagined that I did.

"Will you marry me, Mildred?" I looked up at her from one knee, crouching before her on the corner of a busy street. I hadn't planned this, but then I hadn't planned any of it. It had all just happened. She had just happened...

Holly looks up from the book and stares at the tree again. Jake had just happened for her. He'd applied for a position to leave the Miami P.D. and come to Christmas Key, and when he'd arrived, they'd fallen into an easy pattern of dating and then living together. But had it been as powerful as the feeling in the first paragraph of Uncle Jack's book? She thinks about it for a minute, remembering all the good times they'd had, and ultimately about the way she'd had to turn him down when he'd proposed.

River had just happened, too. He'd shown up a year and a half before with a group of fishermen from Oregon—their first real group of tourists. His fun-loving, impulsive sense of humor and good looks had made falling for him easy. But after some long-distance romance and a trip to Europe that had ultimately ended things for them, Holly had realized that no man so far had been able to hold a candle to her island. There had been a few guys who'd caught her attention in college, sure, but she'd always come home, never once considering leaving Christmas Key permanently for another life. And now, at thirty-one, she's really never known the kind of love that would make someone drop to one knee on a street corner of a major city and ask to have their love for eternity.

Mildred Beaulieu was the most glamorous woman I'd ever seen at the tender age of twenty-six. I'd been hired as waitstaff for an elegant event at the Georgian Terrace hotel on Peachtree Street in Atlanta. All I knew about that night was that I'd be serving champagne for a woman's birthday and that she'd been recently widowed and wanted the evening to be festive.

I'd straightened my bowtie in the mirror over the dirty sink in the men's room behind the kitchen, then walked out into the ballroom carrying a tray of champagne glasses.

"Over here, young man," a woman said, summoning me with one black-gloved hand. I ducked my head and approached.

The woman was talking to a small group of men, holding their attention with a story about a woman who bred horses in the countryside. A few colorful adjectives slipped from her red lips as she spoke, and the men all held smiles on their faces as they anticipated the punchline.

She turned to me without warning as I waited for a man with slick gray hair to take his champagne flute from my tray.

"Have you ever ridden?" she asked me, one perfect eyebrow arched suggestively.

"Uh, horses?" I asked, trying to balance the tray in my hands.

"Yes, darling. Though I'd be willing to bet that you could be broken and ridden by any woman worth her weight in gold."

"Oh, Mildred, leave the boy alone," said the gray-haired man as he took a drink of champagne. "You're old enough to be his mother."

The look in Mildred's eyes shifted from playful to curious. "Am I?" she asked me. "Am I old enough to be your mother?"

I swallowed hard. Talking about a woman's age was always a trick question. I knew this.

I hedged my bets and went for it. "I doubt it. But if you were my mother, I would have misbehaved more and hoped for a good spanking."

The men in the group roared with approving laughter and the woman, who I had yet to realize was the birthday girl, looked at me appraisingly.

"The night is young, sweetheart," she said. "I bet you could still get into enough trouble here for me to spank you." She winked and drained her champagne as the men continued to laugh.

And that was my formal introduction to Mildred Beaulieu, the most glamorous woman I'd ever known. The funniest and most interesting creature to ever walk this earth. The love of my life.

Holly sets her head against the back of the couch and closes her eyes. Jack and Mildred had obviously sparked and made a flame on contact. She'd seen Bonnie fall hard several times for the men who came to Christmas Key, and she'd watched her own grandparents love and care for each other her whole life. True love is out there. She's confident that it exists, and that it doesn't care about things like age or the past, that it cares only for for the two people involved and for their future together.

She reaches down to run her hands over Pucci's silky ears as she watches the lights of the tree for a moment. Then, pulling the blanket more tightly over her legs, she begins to read again.

WHEN HOLLY WAKES UP, THE BOOK HAS FALLEN CLOSED ON HER LAP AND Pucci is snoring loudly on the carpet next to the couch. The lights of the tree are still blinking, and there is the sound of rain against the roof. Holly is disoriented for a moment.

"Pooch," she says, rubbing her eyes. "What time is it?" She throws off the blanket and stands, stretching her arms overhead. Pucci ignores her and keeps snoring, so Holly steps over him.

In the kitchen, the clock on the microwave says 2:09. Holly wraps her arms around her upper body and walks to the window. Rain is pelting the wide fronds of the palm trees outside, and water is streaming down the glass panes. No one had talked about the fact that it might rain, and this turn in the weather has Holly awake and thinking about what she might find in her cupboards to snack on.

There's not much other than a can of soup and half a box of cereal, so Holly pulls out a bowl and grabs the milk from the refrigerator. Besides dog food, she rarely keeps much on hand, preferring to eat on the go and to be around her neighbors instead of alone in her kitchen. But when a girl wakes up at two in the morning, she needs something to snack on before she can climb into her own bed and go back to sleep.

With a bowl filled to the brim with Cheerios and milk, Holly pads over to the table in the corner of the kitchen and sits down. She pulls her feet up onto the chair and starts to shovel cereal into her mouth sleepily. On the table is the pile of mail she'd never finished sorting over the weekend. She flips through the bathing suit catalog and folds over a few of the pages where the models are showcasing bikinis she likes, then tosses it aside.

The unopened letter from Savannah is next in the pile. Holly slides the envelope open and pulls out a piece of paper. She sets the spoon in her bowl and skims the letter from top to bottom with a frown on her tired face. It's from an attorney named Alejandro Cortez.

"My father?" she says out loud when she gets to the bottom of the letter. "My father," she says again, this time as a statement. She leaves the letter on the table and sets her bowl in the sink without emptying it. "*My father.*"

She walks down the hall in a daze and climbs into her bed to the sound of rain.

The letter is laying on the table with its words facing the ceiling and the light from above the stove illuminating the details contained within.

I represent a man who is interested in pursuing DNA confirmation of blood relation. Based on his prior relationship with Coco Baxter, he believes he may be your father.

21

"BUCKHUNTER." HOLLY WALKS INTO JACK FROSTY'S ON TUESDAY around ten a.m. She's wearing overalls with the cuffs rolled up and her Converse, and on her head is her Yankees cap. Her hair hangs in two long braids. "I need to talk to you."

Buckhunter has been setting chairs on the ground and getting things set up for the day. They're the only two people in the place.

He holds up a hand to stop her. "If this is about hiring Maria on full-time as a hostess, then you can turn your cute self right back around and keep on walking."

Holly attempts a smile, but only manages a brief twitch of her mouth. Her sleep was broken and fitful for the few hours she'd spent in her bed, and her mind is racing.

"No, it's not that. I'd never inflict that on you again."

"Thank god."

"It's something else." Holly pulls out a stool at the bar and sits.

"No Springsteen?" Buckhunter nods at the jukebox.

"Not today." Holly sets her woven bag on top of the bar and slides the letter out. She loves coming in and choosing a Springsteen song every time she visits Jack Frosty's, but this time her mind is completely occupied by other things.

Buckhunter's look turns serious as he realizes that his niece has something on her mind. "What's up, kid?"

Holly holds the envelope flat on the bar beneath her palms as she considers how to begin. "I got this letter in the mail. Probably last week sometime, but I just got around to opening everything last night when I couldn't sleep."

"Opening bills in the middle of the night is always a bad idea," Buckhunter says, attempting a joke to lighten the mood. It falls flat. "Sorry, he says, coming around from behind the bar and sitting on the stool next to Holly's. "Go on."

"It's from Savannah."

"Oh?" Buckhunter's eyebrows go up. He was born and raised in Savannah and he knows the city like the back of his hand, but can't imagine where this is going.

"Just read it, please." Holly's hand shakes slightly as she pushes the letter towards him.

Buckhunter hesitates for a moment. "You sure?"

Holly nods.

He pulls the letter out, unfolds it, and reads it silently. When he's finished, he refolds it and puts it back into the envelope. He waits.

"So?" Holly finally prompts.

Buckhunter nods, but still says nothing.

"Do you know anything about this? Why is this from Savannah? I thought my mom grew up in Miami. You're from Savannah. Who is this guy who thinks he's my dad? Why is he contacting me now? What do you think he wants? I'm thirty-one years old. I don't need a father." Her voice wobbles as she spills forth the thoughts that have been racing through her mind since two o'clock in the morning.

"Your mom came to Savannah," Buckhunter finally says. "The summer she got pregnant with you. She came up to stay for a few days."

Holly's face gives away her confusion. "You two can barely stand each other. Why did she go to see you?"

Buckhunter shrugs. "She was sixteen and she wanted to get away from her parents for a little bit. She and my mom got along pretty well." He shrugs again. "Actually, I have no idea. If I had any clue about what goes through Coco's head or what her motives were for anything, I'd consider myself a genius."

"So…" Holly digests this information. "She came up there. Visited you. Got pregnant?"

"I'm not sure about that. I just know it was the same summer she got pregnant. She went out a few times while she was there. Hung out with a girl I worked with in a restaurant a bit."

"Who?"

Buckhunter tips his chin to the ceiling and looks at the unmoving fan above them. "This is a lot of years ago," he says, running a hand over his chin. It makes a bristling sound against his unshaven cheeks.

"Just over thirty years," Holly reminds him.

"I think it was Celine," he finally says. "Or—no—Celia. She went out with Celia and met her brother. I'm not sure what all they did."

"Do you know what their last name was?" Holly asks, already thinking that she might be able to track these people down on social media somehow. It's a long-shot and she knows it, but before she even considers answering this attorney's letter, she'd like to have a better idea of what she's getting into.

"I don't know if I even knew their last name back then. But you know, there is something you could do to solve this mystery a little more easily," Buckhunter says. He rests his hands and elbows on the bar and turns his head to face Holly.

"I don't want to," she says vehemently. "No way."

"I think you're going to have to, Hol. This is coming out of left field, and it's going to gnaw at you if you don't have answers. I know you."

Holly blows out a long breath and puts her hands over the envelope again, pressing it onto the bar. "You're right," she finally says. "But it's a conversation I don't really want to have. *None* of this is anything I want. I don't need it." She turns to look into her uncle's face and her eyes implore him to do something. To make it stop. To undo this letter's arrival and the disruption to her life. But there's nothing he can do, and she knows it.

"Go," Buckhunter says encouragingly. "Go call her and get it over with. Ask her what she remembers."

Holly nods and slides off the bar stool. "Okay," she says. "I'll call Coco."

THE CONVERSATION WITH HER MOTHER ISN'T ONE SHE WANTS TO HAVE IN her office or around anyone else, so Holly drives her golf cart around December Drive, parking it near Snowflake Banks on the southwest part of the island. She pulls out her phone and dials.

"To what do I owe this honor?" Coco says in lieu of a normal greeting.

"Mom," Holly says.

"Mom? Wow...I'm all ears." Coco's voice is disbelieving. Holly rarely calls her by anything but her first name.

"I got a letter from Savannah," she says, not knowing how to start.

"Is that a college friend of yours?" Coco sounds distracted; the background is noisy with voices and activity.

"No," Holly says with annoyance. "The city. I got a letter post-marked from Savannah. Are you busy? Is this a bad time?"

"I'm getting a pedicure," Coco says. "This is fine. So okay, a letter from Savannah. Go on."

"Some attorney says he has a guy wanting me to do a DNA test. He thinks he might be my father."

Silence from the other end of the phone. All Holly can hear is the background noise that carries on around her mother.

"Is my father from Savannah?" Holly ventures, knowing that she's gone too far down this road to turn back now. She hasn't inquired about her father at all since childhood, nor has she spent much time wondering about him. This line of questioning means that she's opening a door that she's never wanted to open, and her heart races in anticipation.

"I spent time in Savannah." Coco says this and then stops.

"Okay, how much time? And when? Is this even a possibility? It must be, or this guy would have never retained an attorney."

"I'm sure you've already spoken to Leo." Coco sounds crisp and accusing, as if this is a personal affront to her that Holly might have gone right to her uncle with questions.

"Of course." She's grown accustomed to her mother calling Buck-hunter by his first name, but no one other than Coco calls him Leo.

"And what did he say?"

"That you spent time with some girl he worked with at a restaurant."

"Mmmm." The noise Coco makes is noncommittal. Not an agree-ment, but not a denial.

"Mom, I need to know." For Holly, this conversation could have easily never happened. She doesn't feel like the mystery of her paternal origins is going to provide her with some missing puzzle piece in her life, and asking her mother who she slept with at sixteen is a question she could have gone to her grave without asking.

"I slept with Celia's brother," she says simply. "She and I went out and explored the city. I met her brother. We went back to Leo's house and...well, you can imagine."

Holly tries to dodge the mental picture that forms in her mind. She shakes her head and squints out at the turquoise water beyond the sand. It's a gorgeous morning, and the unexpected rain the night before has completely vanished, leaving clear skies and a perfect winter day in its wake.

"So how did this guy have any clue I even existed?"

Coco is quiet for a minute. "The internet? Maybe he knows Leo? I have no idea."

"You think he googled you and found out you had a daughter?"

"I have no idea, Holly. The inner workings of men's minds is a complete mystery to me."

"Buckhunter doesn't know him. He could barely remember the name of the guy's sister."

"Mmmm," Coco says again. A woman says something on the

other end of the line. "Listen, I need to finish up here. Are you going to call this lawyer?"

Holly isn't sure what she expected from her mother, but this casual attitude isn't it. "I'm not sure," she says. "Do you mind if I do?"

"Since when have you cared what I do or don't want you to do, Holly?"

Coco has a point. Holly watches as a bird lands near the water and picks at something with its beak. "What was his name?" she asks.

Coco sighs. "Alex. His name was Alex."

"Is he the only possibility?" It's definitely not a question she wants to ask, but she needs to know whether she's looking at a one hundred percent chance that this Alex guy could be her father, or whether there's a window of possibility that he's not.

"Holly," Coco protests.

"Just tell me."

"Fine." Coco sighs again. "There was also Mateo. But it's definitely either Alex or Mateo."

Holly ends the call with the promise to let Coco know what happens, though this is a situation that she had never in her wildest dreams hoped to be in. She puts her phone into her bag and sits there for another thirty minutes, just watching the waves and the birds. At some point she'll make the call to Alejandro Cortez. At some point she'll deal with it. Just not now. She closes her eyes and turns her face to the winter sun. Not right now.

22

IT'S DECEMBER TWENTY-SECOND AND HOLLY STILL HAS THE LETTER IN her purse. She's been carrying it around for three days, trying to decide what to do next. She's asked Buckhunter not to talk to Fiona about it, and she's decided not to even discuss it with Bonnie until she makes a decision. No one else's opinion will sway her on this; once she's made up her mind about whether or not she wants to pursue this, she'll either do it or she won't.

She's in her office when she gets a text from Logan: *Come to the radio station! Check it out!*

This makes Holly smile. Logan's been running up and down Main Street for the past few days, enlisting Jake and Miguel to help him carry things up to the space that he's completely emptied and cleaned, save for the little table he's pushed up to the window so that he can look out on Main Street. Holly closes her laptop and leaves everything as it is. Pucci gets up from the dog bed in the corner and follows her.

"Howdy, Mayor," Cap says as she enters the cigar shop. Pucci lumbers in after her and eyes Marco warily. In return, the bird squawks loudly at them.

"Looks like your feathered friend isn't loving the influx of activity around here," she says, reaching out a hand for Marco to nuzzle with his head. He declines the offer by turning away from her. "Ouch."

"He's just letting me know that he isn't a fan of people coming and going this much. He'll live." Cap puts a cracker near Marco's head and he grabs it gently, turning away to eat it.

"I'm here to check out the station," Holly says, pointing at the stairs in the back.

"It's pretty impressive." Cap gives Marco one more cracker and then follows Holly through the shop. "This guy has everything set up and ready to go. So now we just wait, right?"

"Yeah, he needs to get the FCC to approve it all, but he wanted me to come and check something out now."

"Then by all means, head on up there." Cap picks up a box from a table and sets it on the counter. He pulls a box cutter from a drawer and slices through the tape, then rips it open. The pungent smell of tobacco drifts through the shop. "Aaah," Cap says. "I never get tired of that."

Holly plugs her nose and makes a gagging face. "I'm out of here," she says. Pucci climbs the steps behind her. "Logan? You here?" She knocks at the door before pushing it open.

"Come on in," he says.

Holly stands in the doorway in amazement. Not only has the space been emptied and polished until it shines—even the windows are crystal clear—but it's been filled with equipment and band posters, and a string of holiday lights rings the room. Logan's moved a computer chair in and he's got everything lit up—from Christmas lights to control board.

"Want to see how it works?" he offers.

Holly walks over to the control board and puts her hands on her hips. "I think I remember some of it. Maybe."

Logan reaches down and pets Pucci's head. "Okay, so if we push this button here, we connect to the airwaves. But we can't do that yet." He points out various things you can do and explains the details to Holly as she listens. "I have it all rigged up to that speaker down there," Logan says, standing up and putting his face to the window. "Did you see it when you came in?"

"I saw it when you and Miguel were working on it the other day."

"Yeah, so that will broadcast whatever is on the air out onto Main Street. But there's an easy off switch," he assures her. "So if you don't want me playing music out there all day, I can easily block it and people won't have to hear."

"This is awesome, Logan," Holly says with genuine awe. "Really."

"You want to be the first to play something on our Main Street speaker?" he offers. "It won't go out on the airwaves—it's just hooked up to the speaker for now."

Holly stares at the control panel. "Forgive me for being dumb, but where is all the music?"

Logan spins his chair to the right and taps the keyboard of a laptop. "Right here. Everything is online now."

"Duh." Holly hits her forehead with the heel of her hand. "I don't know why I was still imagining stacks of CDs and records."

"I've never even seen stacks of records." Logan moves the mouse and clicks on a site. "Here. You pick. Anything you like."

Holly steps over Pucci's long body and stands next to Logan, bending over so that she can peer at the computer screen. She thinks of the songs she might want to hear if she were out on Main Street. And then she thinks of all the songs she used to love to hear when she listened to the radio. How excited she'd get when her favorite songs would come on out of the blue. She glances at the street below. There's no one on the sidewalk at the moment, but the decorations are swaying merrily in a light morning breeze. The sky is blue. The lampposts are wrapped in red and white tinsel like tall candy canes.

Holly reaches for the keyboard and taps out the name of a song. It pops up.

"I want this one," she says.

"You got it, boss," Logan says. He selects the song and connects to the speaker on Main Street.

Bing Crosby begins to croon as "I'll Be Home For Christmas" starts to play.

23

By Christmas Eve morning, Holly has made her decision. She rises early in the half-light of dawn and opens the curtains in the bedroom. There's no frost outside, but a light mist gives the impression of a winter morning and she stands there for a moment, looking at the festive holiday lights hanging from the eaves of Buckhunter and Fiona's house next door. As she watches, the light in their kitchen goes on and Buckhunter appears in the window in a white t-shirt. He's filling his coffeepot at the sink.

Holly puts on a pair of fur-lined Uggs and pulls a sweatshirt over her head. She's still in her glasses and hasn't even brushed her hair, but she passes through her kitchen and grabs a holiday mug, heading out the front door and over to her uncle's house.

"Trick or treat," she says, holding out her mug when he opens the door.

"Wrong holiday." Buckhunter motions for her to come in. "Fiona is still asleep."

He closes the door quietly and leads her into the kitchen. The coffee is dripping into the pot and the room smells like apples and cinnamon.

"We made strudel for the potluck," he says, pointing at several pans lined up on the counter. Each is covered by a dish towel and he lifts one, showing Holly their creation.

"Do you think anyone would know the difference if we cut into one now?"

Buckhunter glances at the doorway as if Fiona might appear there. "Probably not." With a wink at his niece, he pulls a knife from the butcher block and slices into the strudel. "Sit. Coffee is almost ready."

Buckhunter sets the coffee pot on a trivet in the center of the table and sets a carton of milk and a container of sugar next to it. He slides into the seat across from Holly's and hands her a slice of apple strudel.

"Merry Christmas, kid," he says, picking up his fork. "What's on your mind?"

Holly takes a forkful of the moist, sweet strudel and puts it in her mouth. She chews thoughtfully before speaking.

"Remember when I thought the big secret you were keeping from me was that *you* were actually my dad?" she finally says.

"I do." Buckhunter picks up the coffee pot and fills both their mugs. He sets it down again and reaches for the milk.

"It really freaked me out." Holly takes the milk from him and pours some into her coffee. "I'd never wanted to know who my father was, and I definitely didn't want to find out that he was living next door to me. Plus you drove me crazy," she adds with a comical eye roll.

"I remember."

"This kind of fell in my lap, you know?" Holly puts a spoonful of sugar into her coffee and stirs it. "Coco told me about Alex and about her other boyfriend at the time, Mateo."

Buckhunter nods thoughtfully. "A real conundrum. I'm sure even she doesn't know which guy it is."

"She said she didn't care if I dug into it."

"Are you thinking of pursuing this?" Buckhunter holds his mug in both hands. He watches Holly's face closely.

Holly takes a sip of her sweetened coffee and sets the mug down.

"I'm going to email the attorney. I'm not sure if having an answer to this will give me something I need in my life or not, but I'm willing to try."

"Is something really missing?"

Holly lifts one shoulder. She focuses her eyes on the window over Buckhunter's kitchen sink, and at the Christmas lights that are still on outside. "Maybe. For a long time I've thought it was love. A man. I thought that was all I was missing. I mean, I've got the island and everything that entails, but there's a part of me that does feel incomplete."

"Could it be your relationship with Coco?"

"That leaves me feeling incomplete? Maybe," Holly says. "But it's always been the way it is, and I fully accept our relationship. I miss my grandparents a lot, so sometimes I think it's that." She drags her fork across the empty plate, picking up strudel crumbs.

"Could just be the natural desire to take stock of your life as you get older," Buckhunter says. He cuts another piece of strudel for himself and one for Holly, setting it on her plate. "Not that thirty-one is 'older,' but you hit milestones and you really start to think, you know?"

"True," Holly says. "True. But I am going to see this through. I have no idea what will happen or why this guy is even interested in knowing me, but I made my decision, and I just wanted to tell you."

"I respect that. And I still haven't told Fiona," Buckhunter assures her.

"Told Fiona what?" A wild-haired Fiona stands in the doorway to the kitchen, rubbing her eyes. She's wearing an open robe over leggings and a t-shirt.

Holly and Buckhunter exchange a look. It's still Holly's story to share, and he waits for her to tell it.

"Want some coffee?" Holly asks her best friend. She gets up from the table and finds a mug for Fiona. "You'll need it if you're going to hear all of this."

Fiona pulls out a chair and waits for Holly to pour her some coffee. "I'm all ears."

"I'm going to take a DNA test," Holly tells her. "I think some guy from Savannah might be my father."

THE EMAIL SHE WRITES LATER THAT MORNING IS BRIEF AND TO THE point. She tells Alejandro Cortez that yes, she will take the DNA test, and yes, she would be interested in finding out whether the man in question is her father. As far as contact in the event that the test is positive, she is unsure about what she wants that to look like. She hits send and closes the laptop, setting it on her kitchen counter.

Bonnie should be leading the charge at the B&B by this point, bossing everyone around and getting things set up in the kitchen. The dining room is already set up for Christmas from the murder mystery weekend, and Cap has agreed to dress up as Santa for Mexi and Mori's amusement, but also to make things more festive for dinner. Holly picks up her phone and checks for messages to make sure no one needs her at the B&B right away. No texts.

With a quick message to Miguel, Holly heads back to her bedroom and digs through the top drawer of her dresser in search of any bikini top and bottom she can find. In the end, she is totally mismatched, as usual, in a yellow top and a pair of bottoms that are covered in red hearts and little rainbows. She shuts the drawer.

The temperature outside has climbed to seventy-three, and while the water isn't nearly as warm as it is in the summer, Holly feels like getting into the surf and floating on her back for a bit. She puts on her flip-flops, grabs a towel, and calls for Pucci to follow.

There's no reason to drive her cart, so she walks the short distance to the sand, kicking off her flip-flops and dropping her towel under a palm tree. There isn't a single cloud in the sky and the sun is almost directly overhead. Without hesitation, Holly wades into the water and fights the urge to turn around and just lay on the sand instead. It's cold, but it feels invigorating. Pucci stops on the sand and watches her like she's lost her mind.

With a little shout that no one can hear, Holly goes in up to her shoulders and then finally dunks her head. She comes out of the water feeling like her skin has been dipped in ice. With a laugh, she lets the water lift her and she floats on her back, staring up at the December sky. She can't hear anything under the water but her own thoughts, so she gives into them completely, letting the idea that she might soon know who her father is drift around her like seaweed.

After a few minutes she stands up to check on Pucci. He's there on the shore, barking and turning in excited circles.

"What's up, boy?" she calls out, shielding her eyes in the midday sun. Someone is waving at her from beneath the palm tree where she's left her shoes and towel. She squints; it's Miguel. She waves back.

He's clearly gotten her text and decided to join her for a Christmas Eve swim. In one swift motion, he pulls off his t-shirt and leaves it with Holly's things, then breaks into a sprint and runs directly into the water without stopping.

Holly laughs and shields herself as the water he kicks up sprays her.

"Merry Christmas, Mayor," Miguel says with a smile, leaping through the water like he's going to capture her and pull her under.

His enthusiasm is contagious—it's youthful and boyish and funny, and she loves it.

"Merry Christmas, Miguel," she says, splashing him back. "I hope Santa gives you a lump of coal in your stocking this year."

"You, too," he says with a smile. "Or maybe a coconut."

They lay on their backs and float in the sun together until it's time to go and get ready for the potluck dinner.

"I brought drinks!" Holly says that evening as she bumps the B&B's kitchen door with her back and it swings open. Her arms are full carrying a box she's ordered from Tinsel & Tidings, and she sets it on the counter as the group of women bustle about prepping potluck dishes.

Maria Agnelli stands on her toes to peer into the box. She whistles. "That's a lot of vodka."

"There's wine, too," Holly says defensively. She swats at Mrs. Agnelli's hand playfully as she reaches for a bottle of Prosecco like she's going to steal it. "I knew nobody wanted to tend bar tonight, so I thought this would work. Plus I knew nobody would want to eat my cooking, so I also spared us all the agony of me bringing a dish to the potluck."

"Good call, sugar." Bonnie starts taking bottles from the box and setting them on the counter.

Her face is made up with red lips and her hair is perfectly coiffed as usual, but something about Bonnie's face looks distracted. Holly is about to ask her what's going on when Idora walks in with a foil covered dish. She stops short in the doorway.

"Oh," Idora says when she spots Mrs. Agnelli. "I just thought I'd drop off my candied yams."

Mrs. Agnelli turns to the counter and needlessly rearranges salt and pepper shakers and bottles of oil and vinegar.

"I'll go now. See you all out there." Idora hands her dish over to Iris Cafferkey.

"Idora," Holly says. She holds out a hand. "Stay and help us. Come on."

Idora straightens her shirt with a two-handed tug. She squares her shoulders and says nothing.

"Yeah, you might as well stay," Mrs. Agnelli says. She turns around to face Idora. "I'm actually glad you're a lesbian."

The air in the room goes still. Mrs. Agnelli is a firecracker with no filter, but no one had expected her to just come out with it and address the elephant in the room.

Idora arches an eyebrow. "Why? You aren't my type."

There's a pause while everyone decides whether to laugh or not.

"Well," Mrs. Agnelli finally says. "We've already got one man-hungry floozy on the island," she hooks a thumb in Bonnie's direction, "and not enough men to go around. So I'm just glad you're into women."

Holly is sure that this is where she should step in and say something so the candied yams don't go flying, but instead, something strange happens: the two women smile. And then laugh.

"I feel like I should be more insulted," Bonnie says to Holly, but she's laughing along with Idora and Mrs. Agnelli and everyone else.

"Come on." Holly takes Bonnie by the elbow and they escape the kitchen. "I want to hear what's going on."

"What do you mean?" Bonnie follows her to the lobby. They stand by the front window and look at the way Main Street is lit up in the dark.

"You look like your cat just died."

"You know I'm not a cat person." Bonnie folds her arms and looks at the lights across the street.

"You're also not usually this glum." Holly isn't going to stop until she gets to the bottom of things. "So what gives?"

"Oh, just me being an old fool again."

"Stop that, Bon. You're not old and you're not a fool." Holly puts an arm around Bonnie and gives her a playful shake.

"Jantzen hasn't called me back in three days. So I googled him."

"Uh oh." Nothing good comes of Bonnie in a dark mood. Her internal setting is always switched to "cheerful and bubbly," but when things shift...Holly can't even stand to think of it. It's just unnatural. "What did you come up with?"

"Pictures of him and some woman author at an event last month. They looked cozy."

"Well, that was last month," Holly says. Relief floods through her on Bonnie's behalf.

"It said she was his fiancée."

"Ohhhh."

"Why does this always happen to me?" Bonnie is still looking at the lights outside as Gwen and her husband walk through the front door.

"Merry Christmas!" Gwen says as she passes through with a basket in her hands. "I'll run the dinner rolls to the kitchen," she tells her husband, giving him a light shove towards the dining room.

Holly turns back to Bonnie. "Maybe they broke up last month?" she offers gently. "Did you two talk at all about stuff like that? Whether you were both free?"

Bonnie shakes her head. "I just figured if he was spending the weekend with me, he was available."

Holly nods. She can see both of their faces reflected in the window in front of them. "Well, I think you should wait to draw any conclusions until you talk to him."

"I guess. But why hasn't he called in three days?"

"Family in town for the holidays?" Holly suggests.

"We'll see." Bonnie finally loosens her arms from around her own body and reaches out to grab Holly's hand. "Now what's up with you, sugar? I feel like you've been carrying something around for days. Don't think I'm so lost in my man drama that I can't see past the end of my own nose," she adds.

Holly takes a deep breath. She's kept the whole attorney thing to herself and Buckhunter and Coco, and telling Fiona that morning was the first time she'd breathed a word of it to anyone who wasn't family. She hangs onto Bonnie's hand and holds it tighter.

"I got a letter from an attorney in Savannah," she says.

"Ooooh, I love Savannah."

"Well, he isn't inviting me up for a visit," Holly says wryly. "He's inviting me to take a DNA test to confirm whether or not some guy is my father."

Bonnie's face goes from expectant to shocked. "Are you serious?"

Holly turns to look at her. "Yeah. I thought about it for a few days, and I'm going to do it."

"Whoa. Sugar. That's huge. You've never even talked about who your father might be. It just seemed like you didn't need to know."

"I never have," Holly says. "And I wanted to think it through before I emailed this guy, which I did this morning. So I guess we'll see what happens."

"What does Coco say? Won't she just tell you who the guy was?"

"That's part of the problem. She had a boyfriend in Miami at the time named Mateo, but she took a trip up to Savannah that same summer to see Buckhunter and his mom—"

"Wait, are you serious? She went to visit the half-brother she barely acknowledges and the woman who got pregnant with him by her married father?"

"Yeah, I don't quite know the details on that—she didn't give me the how or why, just said she was up there for a few days. And while she was there, she slept with some guy named Alex."

"Oh, dear." Bonnie pats her hair and flutters her eyelashes. For as many men as she's known and loved, there's something slightly unsavory to her proper Southern ideals about not knowing who the father of one's baby is.

"Yeah, but hey, it's only two guys, right?" Holly says dryly. "So I've got a fifty-fifty chance of hitting the jackpot with Mr. Savannah, who I'm assuming is Alex."

"Lordy, lordy, child." Bonnie makes a tsk-tsk sound with her tongue. "What are you going to do when you find out it's him?"

Holly hasn't thought this far—at least not in concrete terms. She knows that having the information will give her some sort of peace of mind, but as to whether she'll go and visit him or invite him down to the island—or whether someday they might meet up in neutral territory—none of that has been decided just yet.

"I have no idea. I'm just taking things as they come. And you should, too." Holly bumps Bonnie's hip with her own. "We don't have all the answers, so we shouldn't rush to judgment just yet, huh?"

A small smile plays at Bonnie's lips. "You're right, doll. And it's Christmas."

Holly turns and puts both hands on Bonnie's shoulders so that they're facing each other. "Having you safe is the best present I'm going to get this year," she says. The memory of Bonnie missing in the water is still something that flashes through her mind each day, filling her with fresh horror every time she thinks of it.

Bonnie's eyes are watery as she looks at Holly. "Oh, sugar. What did I ever do to deserve you?"

They stand like that for a moment as the noise from the dining room surrounds them. Someone has turned on the music and there is laughter and talk as everyone exchanges Christmas greetings.

"Get in here, you two!" Fiona pokes her head into the doorway of the lobby. "Dinner is served!"

Holly and Bonnie hold hands and follow Fiona into the dining room, which looks as magical as it had on the first night of the murder mystery. Holly stops short as Mexi chases Mori past them, nearly tripping her as they hold up little plastic airplanes like they're flying them through the air.

"Sorry, ladies!" Calista says to them, following her boys and trying to curb their enthusiasm.

"No need to be sorry," Bonnie assures her. "I've raised a few boys myself. They've gotta get that energy out somewhere —trust me."

Calista smiles at them over her shoulder as she follows the twins.

Wyatt is standing near a table with his hands on the back of a chair. He raises a hand. "I saved you a seat, Bonnie," he says, pulling out the chair.

Holly lets go of Bonnie's hand. "Looks like someone's Christmas wish is to have dinner with Ms. Lane," she says into Bonnie's ear. "See you at the buffet table."

With Bonnie making her way over to Wyatt's table, Holly walks through the room solo, greeting everyone as she goes. She pauses at the table where Katelynn is sitting next to her grandfather.

"Hi," Holly says. "Good to see you here tonight, Hal. Merry Christmas, Katelynn."

Hal gives Holly a smile that tells her he recognizes her, even if he can't quite find her name. "Hello, young lady," he says hoarsely.

"Have you heard about your great-grandson's project?" she asks Hal, leaning over so that he can hear her. "He's got all your old radio equipment set up above North Star Cigars."

"Yes," Hal says. He raises one shaky finger in the air. "And I like it when a young person has a project. Keeps them busy and out of trouble."

"Agreed." Holly smiles at him. "You kept me busy with that same equipment when I was young, *and* you got me hooked on music. I loved every minute of it."

Hal's eyes are faraway, like he's trying to imagine the scene she's talking about. Rather than put him on the spot by asking him to recall any of that time, Holly stands up straight and looks around. "Where are Jake and Logan?" she asks Katelynn.

Katelynn tips her head towards the buffet. "Loading up their plates, of course. You know how guys are when they see a table full of food."

Holly laughs. "Naturally. And Iris made her famous Christmas stuffing, so I'm sure they'll be heading over there multiple times."

Cap gives Holly a gloved salute from Santa's throne. He's dressed in a red velvet suit and a big white beard that covers most of his face. Holly marvels over the fact that little kids can't tell when someone they know is dressed up as Santa, but Mexi and Mori run up to sit on his knee with faces full of awe and wonder. It seems as though they have no clue that it's someone they see everyday hiding behind the beard.

"Crazy, isn't it?" Vance appears at her side and they watch the boys together. "Two hellions like these kids are totally tamed by Cap Duncan in a Santa costume." He shakes his head. "How are you doing, Holly? I haven't talked to you much since the murder mystery weekend."

"I've been busy," she says, tearing her gaze away from the boys as each perches on one of Cap's knees. He's making exaggerated faces at them as Calista snaps photos on her iPhone. "How about you? Did you sell a ton of Jantzen Parks books while he was here?"

"A fair amount," Vance says. "And a bunch of other stuff, too."

"Excellent. I feel like the weekend went really well for all of us—lots of tourist dollars floating around, if you want to get down to the nuts and bolts of it."

"All business owners want to get down to the nuts and bolts of it." Vance crosses his arms over his lean chest. "And I heard you had some ideas for a website where we might be able to sell things. I'd definitely like to hear more about that."

"I'm working on it," Holly says. "Mostly in my head at this point, but I'm going to talk more about it at the next village council meeting."

"Sounds good." Vance watches his wife and kids for a moment. "Hey, how'd it go with that book that Bonnie had me track down for you? Something about her uncle who wrote a book about her aunt?"

"Oh, I'm still reading it. It's actually really good."

"Seriously?" Vance's eyebrows shoot up. "I'm always surprised when something like that ends up being worth reading. A lot of books that are just family history are only meant for the people who know and love the author and subject."

"No, I'm loving it. I just got sidetracked and put it down for a couple of days, but I'm going to binge it tonight and tomorrow and hopefully get through it completely. I'm fascinated by Bonnie's aunt and uncle and their love story."

"Well, let me know how it turns out, will you?"

"Will do." Holly spots Fiona and Buckhunter at a table on one side of the room. "I'll talk to you later, Vance. I hope Santa brings the boys everything they want this year."

Vance laughs. "These spoiled boys don't need anything other than what they have. But I'm sure he'll treat them right. Enjoy the book."

Holly wanders around the room, chatting with friends and neighbors as they tuck into food from the buffet. So much has happened since the previous Christmas Eve. Just one year before, River had been on the island visiting for the holidays, and Holly had awoken to find him looking pensive and needing to talk. He'd decided to leave the island that morning and to put the brakes on their relationship, and Holly had ended up spending that evening at the chapel with her neighbors. Jake was dating Bridget, the actress he'd met on the set of *Wild Tropics*, and things had been in a state of flux.

But this year feels more concrete. Jake and Katelynn are sitting at a table together, talking over glasses of red wine. Holly hasn't spoken to River in a while, but she's come to grips with the fact that they tried something and got everything out of it that they could. And what more can you do when it comes to love than give it your best shot?

She glances at Wyatt and Bonnie, who is laughing heartily at something he's just said. The candlelight catches Bonnie's face just right, enhancing her loveliness and making her look as happy as Holly's ever seen her.

It's a good feeling, being amongst the people she loves most on her favorite holiday. Holly wouldn't trade this moment for anything in the world.

24

SHE RARELY SEES THE INSIDE OF FIONA'S DOCTOR'S OFFICE, BUT ON Christmas morning, Holly sits on the paper covered exam table, hands folded in her lap.

"Let's just do it before I have time to overthink things," she says, watching as Fiona pulls out a swab and the other things she'll need to get a cheek sample for the DNA test. "Are you sure you have everything?"

"I'm sure," Fiona says patiently. Holly had stayed up until almost three o'clock reading Uncle Jack's book the night before, then slept a few hours before texting Fiona to see if she'd be willing to do the test that day. "This is pretty easy. Open wide."

Holly obeys and Fiona sticks the long swab in, scraping it against the side of Holly's cheek.

"Ah oo gah duh da?" Holly says around the giant Q-tip in her mouth.

Fiona pulls it out with an amused smile. "What was that?"

"I said, what are you guys doing today?" Holly swipes at her mouth with the back of one hand. "Got any big Christmas plans?"

"I was just going to sleep in," Fiona says.

"I'm sorry! I woke you!" Holly's hands fly to her mouth.

"Nah, it's okay. Honestly." Fiona puts the DNA sample in a bag and then bends over her counter to fill out a form with Holly's information. "I was actually awake before Buckhunter for once, and I was just going to wrap one more present for him. Hey," she says, turning around, "you want to come over and do presents with us?"

It's on the tip of Holly's tongue to accept without hesitation, but then she remembers that this is Fiona and Buckhunter's first Christmas as husband and wife, and something holds her back. They deserve to have their own traditions and holiday routines.

"Nah, you two enjoy your day together. This is your time. You don't need your husband's spinster niece tagging along all the time."

Fiona snorts. "Spinster? You're thirty-one, Hol. That's not exactly spinster territory. And we'd love to have you."

Holly smiles at Fiona's back. She knows her best friend is being honest: they would have her over for the holiday and she wouldn't for one second be made to feel like an interloper. But for some reason, she wants to spend this day doing her own thing.

"Actually, I think I'm going to keep reading. I might go to the beach or something. And I know Joe is opening up the Ho Ho later on, so I'll probably head over there."

"You still reading the book about Bonnie's aunt and uncle?"

"Yeah. I stayed up really late reading it last night, but I fell asleep around three. That keeps happening: I get into bed with the book, then wake up with it on my lap. Got anything you can prescribe to keep an old lady awake, Doc?"

"More sleep," Fiona says as she folds the paper and slides it into an envelope with the cheek swab. "You burn the midnight oil and then work your tail off all day running from one side of this island to the other. Something's gotta give."

"So you're saying that it's unreasonable for me to stay up all night reading after working all day?"

"Fairly unreasonable. Plus you exist on coffee and snacks for fuel. When's the last time you cooked anything in your own kitchen?"

"Ummmm." Holly turns her eyes to the ceiling, pretending to calculate. "Maybe March?"

"Girl. You need to practice some self-care. Maybe that should be your New Year's resolution."

"To learn to cook?" Holly slides off the table and stands.

"To make real food for yourself. To get enough sleep. To take more walks on the beach and spend less time racing around and worrying about everyone and everything."

Holly looks at the concern in Fiona's eyes. Her friend only has her best interests at heart, and she knows it. "I do have some fun. Yesterday Miguel and I went swimming before the potluck. That was relaxing."

Fiona tries to keep her face neutral, but a twitch of her mouth and a hitch of one eyebrow betrays her. "Oh?"

"Yeah, yeah, yeah," Holly says, rolling her eyes. "I know. I went swimming with Miguel."

Fiona shrugs. "I'm not saying anything about that. I think Miguel is great and I love seeing how happy you are when you two are hanging around each other."

"We do have a good time. He's funny and easygoing."

Fiona waits for more. When Holly says nothing, she clears her throat. "Well, as your best friend and your doctor, I have to ask: do we need to talk about some sort of birth control?"

"Fee!" Holly blushes.

"That's a perfectly reasonable question." Fiona isn't the least bit flummoxed by doctor talk. "And there aren't many women on the island who need me to talk birth control with them, so if you need something, I want to make sure I have it on hand."

Holly sits on the table again and crosses her feet at the ankles. Her flip flops dangle a few inches from the floor. "Fiona," she says gravely. "I need your honest opinion."

"Okay. Professional or personal?" Fiona sets her stethoscope on the counter and leans against the ledge with one hip.

"Personal."

"Okay, shoot."

"This is totally confidential, of course."

"Of course." Fiona gives a single nod.

"Do you think the age difference between me and Miguel is completely ridiculous? That it makes me look like..."

"A cougar?" Fiona finishes for her.

"Exactly."

"No, I don't think so. We're talking about, what—six or seven years here?"

"Eight," Holly says reluctantly. "He's only twenty-three."

Fiona takes a long pause to think it through before answering. "Eight years?" she says. "And you're both adults?"

Holly can see where Fiona is going with this, so she waits.

"I think eight years is nothing, in the grand scheme of things. Now, is there a difference in life experience between twenty-three and thirty-one? Sure. Is it insurmountable? Absolutely not."

Holly chews on her lower lip as she listens. Her eyes are on the poster of the human skeleton that hangs on the back of Fiona's exam room door.

"But do you think it's possible to find something real with someone when there's a noticeable age gap between you?"

"Holly," Fiona says, lowering her chin. She stares at her best friend as if she's climbed out from under a rock with half her brain missing. "How many years are there between me and Buckhunter?"

Realization dawns on Holly and her face completely changes. "Oh! Fee, oh my god!"

"Right?" Fiona watches Holly as the mental math starts to compute.

"Eight years," Holly says.

"Eight years," Fiona confirms. "Which means that when he was thirty-one..."

"You were twenty-three."

"Now does that mean we would have met each other and fallen in love at those ages? I have no idea." Fiona turns her palms to the ceiling. "But when you connect with someone, that barely matters. In fact, I kind of think it doesn't matter at all. No more than the color of your skin, which church you go to, or how tall you are."

"I'm so dumb." Holly presses the heel of her hand to her fore-head. "Honestly."

"You're not dumb—you're cautious. There's a difference." Fiona stares at her. "And you have a right to be."

"But the fact that I've taken a few extra trips around the sun doesn't actually make that much difference, does it?"

"Not in my opinion." Fiona pushes herself away from the counter and walks over to the exam table. She sits on it so that her shoulder is touching Holly's. "Does he make you laugh?"

"Yes."

"Does he make you feel important?"

Holly laces her fingers together in her lap. "Mmmhmm."

"And most importantly, do you *feel* like there's something there? A connection?"

After a pause, Holly turns her head and looks at Fiona. "Yeah. There's something. I've wished a few times that he would just kiss me so we could see if there was really a spark. But then in the next breath I've hoped he wouldn't so that nothing would change between us."

"Things always change, Hol. For better or worse. That's kind of the name of the game."

"So you're saying I should just kiss him and see what happens?"

"Maybe more metaphorically than literally," Fiona says. She bumps Holly's shoulders with her own. "More like just take it as it comes. See what happens. Don't set so many rules and limitations on yourself."

"Eight years is nothing," Holly says, almost as if she's trying to convince herself.

"When it really comes down to it, eight years is nothing," Fiona echoes.

Holly slides off the table and straightens the waistband of her sweatpants. She's barely gotten out of bed and hasn't even officially dressed for the day yet.

"Thanks, Fee," she says. "For doing the DNA test and for the advice." She reaches out and puts her hand on the doorknob.

"You'll let me know about that birth control, right?" Fiona gets off the exam table and pulls the paper off of it, replacing it with a fresh sheet for the next patient.

Holly pulls the door open and turns back to smile at Fiona. "Merry Christmas, Fee," she says. "Tell Buckhunter I said thanks for letting me borrow you for a little bit."

"You got it, girl. Merry Christmas."

25

There's no one staying at the B&B, so Holly decides to spend Christmas Day there pretending like she lives in a hotel just like Eloise at The Plaza. She's brought a bikini, the book by Uncle Jack, her cell phone, and Pucci. They walk through the quiet hallway together as Holly flips on lights and chooses a room to use as her own.

"Should we call for room service, Pooch?" she asks, sitting on the foot of the bed in the Palm Tree Pagoda. Pucci looks at her from his spot near the door as if he already knows she's kidding.

Holly flops back on the bed and looks around the room like a guest might, trying to see things through the eyes of someone visiting for the first time. The walls are covered in a textured rattan wallpaper that's meant to mimic the trunk of a palm tree, and the nightstands are wicker and glass. The four-poster bed has a lemon yellow duvet cover and throw pillows shaped like pineapples. The lamps on the bedside tables have round bases that look like sea glass and crisp, white shades. It's one of Holly's favorite rooms.

She takes her book and wanders through the empty halls, not even bothering to close the door to her room. The kitchen is lit only from the sunlight that spills through the windows, so Holly flips on the overheads and sets her book on the counter. In the fridge are plenty of leftovers from the night before.

There's a radio on the window sill and Holly turns it on low; she's getting Christmas carols from a station in Miami. With the small portion of ham that's left, two dinner rolls, and a pot of dijon mustard from the refrigerator, Holly makes herself mini sandwiches and sets them on a plate.

She hasn't even bothered to call Bonnie or Miguel to see what they're doing today, and as she sticks the side of her thumb in her mouth to lick the stray mustard from it, she wonders if she should invite people to join her. Her cell phone is in her back pocket and she could easily call someone and say, "Hey, come on over to the B&B and help me eat leftovers." But something stops her. There's nothing wrong with being alone, and there isn't one part of Holly that feels sorry for herself about flying solo on Christmas Day. After all, she's got a whole hotel to herself, and she's got bowls of Maria Agnelli's cold pasta and Bonnie's pink ambrosia salad. She glops a generous helping of each onto her plate with a serving spoon before recovering the dishes with plastic wrap and putting them back in the fridge.

After grabbing a fork, a napkin, and a can of Diet Coke, Holly puts everything on a tray—including her book—and backs out through the swinging door, leaving the radio on behind her. Pucci is waiting patiently in the hallway (he's always been afraid of swinging doors, and he prefers to park himself just outside and wait whenever Holly enters the kitchen) and together they make their way to the pool deck.

The sun is climbing in the sky as Holly chooses a chair to lounge in and sets up her little feast on the table next to her. The temperature has climbed into the low 70s and she kicks off her flip flops and gets comfortable with her book in her lap. Pucci curls up under a table with an umbrella and promptly falls asleep.

Holly cracks her book and starts to read.

That night, Mildred Beaulieu was on stage in a community production of The Best Little Whorehouse in Texas, dressed like Mae West. I sat back in my seat in the front row, trying to stifle my amusement and growing arousal.

As the chorus began to sing behind her and the lights shone on her smiling face, Mildred flipped open her fan and put it in front of her mouth, looking down at me with only her eyes. She kept them on me for just a beat too long and when she dropped her fan and started to sing again, I knew with absolute certainty that there'd be no other woman in my life. Not now, not ever.

Behind the thick, dusty red curtains was a backstage area filled with women of all ages and sizes in stage makeup and corset-type costumes that had been cinched up tight. The overall effect was that their torsos and bottoms ended up looking like hearts and upside down hearts, respectively. It made the air feel thick with lusty womanhood.

"Mildred," I said, approaching her from behind. In my hands were a dozen red roses, which I held out to her shyly. She glanced at my offering and then back up at my face.

"You came," she said. A smile played at her lips that told me she'd known all along I'd be there.

"If a beautiful woman invites you to watch her onstage singing and dancing, you show up," I said, thrusting the flowers at her. She took them and held them to her nose, inhaling deeply.

"Are we still pretending I'm your mother?" she asked, looking at me with just her eyes and keeping the flowers in front of her face the same way she'd done with the fan onstage.

"I never for one second imagined that you were my mother," I said firmly. "Now go and change so I can take you out for a drink."

It was a calculated gamble, talking to her like that, but she paused for just a moment, smiled appreciatively, and then turned to make for the dressing rooms. I found a chair in a corner and sat.

Actors and actresses streamed past me as I waited, laughing and talking excitedly about the little mistakes they'd made or the successes they'd had as they'd torn through the scenes and the songs. I smiled at the younger women, waiting for my eyes to caress their bare calves and accentuated backsides in the short costumes. Surely my usual desire to appreciate a woman's ripe form would take over, and soon I'd be looking at some sweet girl in her twenties, wondering what it would take to be the one to unlace her corset in a dressing room and free her from the bondage of her tight bustier. But it never happened. In my mind, all I could think of was Mildred on the stage, her shapely legs ending in a pair of high-heeled dance shoes, her eyes watching me with risk and desire.

That night we drank standing up at tall tables in a dark bar, her every smile a challenge, her every touch an invitation. I ended the evening by pulling her close under a streetlight, the world wobbling around us as I held her and swayed, humming "Unforgettable" in her ear. She smelled faintly of sweet perspiration and of the stage makeup she'd mostly washed off. I wanted to know what her whole body smelled like: the folds where her ribcage met her arms; the crease beneath her breasts; the flesh of her taut stomach. It was a desire unlike any that I'd ever felt for a woman. It was an animal-like need to inhale her, to bring her close, to turn the molecules of her into something I could carry with me long after she'd gone. I wanted her to meld into me the way stars had once imploded and fallen to earth, ingested by humans and turned into our skeletons and hearts, reborn again and again with each generation.

Quite simply, I wanted her—all of her.

We were never apart after that—not even for one night. If I spent twenty-four hours a day with her, I'd fall asleep wishing that a day had twenty-five hours so I could have just a little more time with the woman I loved. Hours and days and years became a theme for us, as we both knew in our hearts that there would never be enough time for us. We banned any morbid talk of the inevitable, instead focusing on the here and now at all times.

But sometimes—in the dark, lying under a sheet with our fingers and bodies intertwined—it would come up. How would I live without her? How could I possibly go on? What might I think when her fifties ended and her face began to change like a time-lapse photo? Would I look at her one day and think, "Who is this? And why do I love her?" Or would I always see in her the sexy, headstrong woman who'd demanded to celebrate her first birthday as a widow with champagne and laughter, offering to spank me in front of a group of men three times my age?

I couldn't think about it—I refused to acknowledge in the light of day that I might one day have to live without the woman who thought me perfect and desirable and funny. I wouldn't answer her questions about what I would do when she was gone. All I would tell her as the light of the moon played shadow tricks in the darkened bedroom was that I would love her forever. That she was the most amazing woman I'd ever known. That her heart was her real treasure—not her physical beauty, though I loved that, too. And I meant it all. Every single word. I still do.

Holly sets the book facedown on the chair next to her feet and picks up her can of Diet Coke. It opens with a satisfying crack of the tab. Above the palm trees that line the pool deck the sky is blue and dotted with lazy clouds. Even though the weather is mild and she's in shorts and a t-shirt, it still feels like winter. And—more than that—in spite of being surrounded by reminders of the holidays year-round, it actually feels like Christmas.

She and Bonnie and Miguel have hung oversize ornaments from the lower branches of the palm trees around the pool, and the fence that surrounds the area is decorated with lights. She could spend the whole day right here with Pucci and her book, then head inside and watch a movie in the big bed of the Palm Tree Pagoda in the fluffy white robe that's hanging in the closet of her suite. She's pretty sure she can even track down some popcorn in the B&B's kitchen and that there's still enough holiday candy laying around to keep her busy though at least one showing of *White Christmas* and possibly even *Elf*.

But her mental plans are interrupted by a knock at the gate.

"Ho, ho, ho," says a deep voice. "There's a Puerto Rican Santa here to grant all your Christmas wishes."

Holly swings her feet around and stands up on the concrete patio. "Hold your horses there, Santa," she says, walking over to the gate and unlatching it. "Come on in."

"What are you doing here all alone?" Miguel says, looking around to make sure that she is, in fact, on her own.

Holly shrugs. "Just chilling out. Having a little solo Christmas celebration. I'm reading and eating leftovers," she says, nodding at her spot near the pool.

"Oh, gotcha. Want me to leave you to it?" Miguel's hair is damp from a recent shower, and even from a foot or two away, Holly can smell his soap and shaving cream. Every time he comes near her, she finds herself inadvertently breathing in and holding it, and once or twice she's been sure he's noticed.

"No, come in, come in." She waves him through the gate and closes it quickly as if someone might be watching. "You smell nice."

Miguel is light on his feet as he turns to her with a curious look. "What do I smell like?"

Holly hesitates only slightly before leaning closer and breathing in, as she always wants to do. "You smell like..." She breathes out deeply. "Like spicy Christmas trees."

"Like spicy Christmas trees?" he laughs. "Where in the world have you smelled a spicy Christmas tree?"

Holly puts her hands together and points at his neck with both index fingers. "Right there," she says.

"Oh, right here?" Miguel takes a big step closer so that he's now just inches from Holly. "Better come here and confirm that. I want to make sure that's actually true before I put it on my resumé."

"You're putting that on your resumé?" Holly smiles at him as he takes hold of both her wrists and brings her even closer. "That you smell like spicy Christmas trees?"

"I might," Miguel says quietly as he looks into her eyes. "If it's something you like, then it's worth noting."

Holly can feel her own heart beating wildly as he draws near, and she can see his pulse throbbing beneath the tan skin of his neck. *Spicy Christmas trees*, she thinks dizzily, nearly drowning in the scent of him. *My new favorite smell.*

"So what are you reading?" Miguel asks softly, his lips dangerously close to her ear.

"A book that Bonnie's uncle wrote about the torrid love affair he had with her late aunt."

"And what made it so torrid?" Miguel takes a step away from Holly and tries to read the cover of the book from where they stand.

"Um," Holly chews on the inside of her cheek. "Well."

"Well what? She was born a man? He already had four wives?"

Holly shifts her weight from one foot to the other. "She was older than him."

"Hmm," Miguel says. "How much?"

"Thirty-two years."

"Wait, what?" Miguel laughs. "Are you serious?"

"Yeah." Holly doesn't smile. "But in the end, it didn't matter. They were crazy about each other."

Miguel's face turns serious. "That's all that ever matters, in my opinion. If two people like each other, then the rest is just details."

Holly stares at the book and then at Pucci, who barely lifts his head to acknowledge Miguel's arrival. "You think so?"

"I know so."

There's a pause as they look at each other meaningfully.

"Hey," Holly says. "Are you hungry?"

"Starving."

"I've got a kitchen full of leftovers, and I was about to watch a Christmas movie in the Palm Tree Pagoda. Want to join me?"

"A—yes to the leftovers. And B—what movie?"

"What sounds good?" Holly picks up her plate of food and whistles for Pucci to follow them.

"Can we watch *Elf*?"

"Oh, Miguel," Holly says, holding the door to the lobby open with one foot and balancing her plate of food in her hand. "You smell good *and* you have solid taste in holiday movies. I like that."

"You gonna keep me around?" Miguel takes the plate from her and leads the way into the B&B.

"I think I might," Holly says, giving one last look at the empty pool deck that's ringed with Christmas lights. "I really think I might."

YOU JUST FINISHED BOOK SIX OF THE CHRISTMAS KEY SERIES! DOWNLOAD BOOK SEVEN, *POLISH THE STARS*, TO FIND OUT WHAT HAPPENS NEXT!

READY FOR THE NEXT BOOK IN THE CHRISTMAS KEY SERIES?

When a tragedy happens on the island its residents must pull together to help a stranger--whether they agree with Holly's methods and motives or not. Join Christmas Key's colorful locals for another adventure as they navigate life and love on an island wrapped in tinsel and twinkling lights! Buy it here!

ABOUT THE AUTHOR

Stephanie Taylor is a high-school teacher who loves sushi, "The Golden Girls," Depeche Mode, orchids, and coffee. Together with her teenage daughter she writes the *American Dream* series—books for young girls about other young girls who move to America. On her own, Stephanie is the author of the *Christmas Key* books, a romantic comedy series about a fictional island off the coast of Florida.

https://redbirdsandrabbits.com
redbirdsandrabbits@gmail.com

ALSO BY STEPHANIE TAYLOR

To see a complete list of the Christmas Key series along with all of
Stephanie's other books, please visit:

Stephanie Taylor's Books

To hear about any new releases, sign up here and you'll be the first to know!

Made in the USA
Columbia, SC
19 October 2023

24674337R00121